THE
WHITE
ZONE

THE WHITE ZONE

CAROLYN MARSDEN

CAROLRHODA BOOKS
MINNEAPOLIS

Carolrhoda Books
A division of Lerner Publishing Group, Inc.
241 First Avenue North
Minneapolis, MN 55401 U.S.A.

Website address: www.lernerbooks.com

The image in this book is used with the permission of: Front Cover: © John
R. Kreul/Independent Picture Service.

Main body text set in Janson Text LT Std 12/17.
Typeface provided by Linotype AG.

Library of Congress Cataloging-in-Publication Data

Marsden, Carolyn.
       The White Zone / by Carolyn Marsden.
          p.   cm.
       Summary: As American bombs fall on Baghdad during the Iraq War,
ten-year-old cousins Nouri and Talib witness the growing violence
between Sunni and Shiite Muslims.
       ISBN: 978–0–7613–7383–4 (trade hard cover : alk. paper)
          1. Iraq War, 2003—Juvenile fiction. [1. Iraq War, 2003—Fiction.
2. Muslims—Fiction. 3. Violence—Fiction. 4. Cousins—Fiction.
5. Baghdad (Iraq)—Fiction. 6. Iraq—Fiction.] I. Title.
PZ7.M35135Wj 2012
[Fic]—dc23   2011021227

Manufactured in the United States of America
1 – SB – 12/31/11

FOR PAL

WINTER

BLACK CAR, WHITE COFFIN

Nouri covered his eyes against a blast of blowing sand.

When the gust had passed, he opened his eyes to the al-Salam cemetery. Stretching as far as he could see, the flat ground was punctuated by the tombs of the Shiite prophets. The air was cold and Nouri shivered in his new black suit.

In the distance, the glittering gold dome and minarets of the mosque rose into the dusty sky. But Nouri stared only at the white coffin beside the hole in the earth where his uncle would soon be locked away forever. Never again would he smile at Nouri or kick a soccer ball his way.

When the market had been attacked last week by the Sunni martyr, thirty-four people had died. Nouri's uncle had been among the dead.

As the white coffin was lowered into the ground, Mama and A'mmo's other female relatives slapped their faces and wailed in grief.

Nouri's younger cousins, Anwar and Jalal, remained dry-eyed. They were busy bouncing a small rubber ball behind the backs of the grown-ups.

Nouri hoped his cousins wouldn't see the tears wetting his cheeks. Anwar and Jalal hadn't been as close to Mama's youngest brother as he had. They'd never gone with A'mmo to the glassy building in the Green Zone where he worked as a bank teller. They'd never ridden in his black car, which was small, but very shiny.

Nouri had loved that car almost as much as he loved his uncle. Even though the corner store was an easy walk away, A'mmo always drove him there to buy pencils and candies. The kids of the neighborhood had circled the shiny black exterior, running their fingertips over the chrome.

Now everything was different. Baba had driven the family to A'mmo's funeral in that car, traveling the three hours to Najaf City from Baghdad.

Gradually, A'mmo Hakim's relatives made their way to the line of cars that had driven in the convoys from Baghdad and Mosul.

While Mama leaned in to kiss her relatives on both cheeks, Nouri bit his cheeks against the tears building in his throat. A'mmo Hakim was really gone.

Mama climbed into the front seat of the black car and Nouri got in next to the back window. His little sister. Shatha—a large black bow in her hair—scooted to the middle, making room for Mama's sister.

A'mmo Hakim's once-shiny car was dusty now. Tomorrow, Nouri told himself, he'd get up early to clean it. He'd make this car his. Surely, since he'd been A'mmo's favorite nephew, A'mmo would want him to have it.

Nouri wouldn't be able to drive the car for years and years, but he knew it would be waiting.

As they drew closer to Baghdad, the sky ahead burned with the green flash of tracer fire. Explosions rocked the night. Baba drove straight into that war, the one they lived with every day.

As they passed a group of motorcycles stuck behind a horse-drawn cart, Baba patted the steering wheel and said, "We should get a good price for this car."

Nouri leaned forward to hear better, pushing against his sister, who elbowed him back. How could Baba *suggest* such a thing?

"You'd sell it right away?" Mama lifted her arm, her bracelets jingling.

"Why not? We need the money."

"It's something to remember Hakim by. . . ." Mama's voice trailed off.

Mama was right—the car was all they had left of A'mmo Hakim. "We could use this car," Nouri said firmly.

Baba shook his head. "Cars cost money to keep. Buses are good enough."

Nouri leaned back, breathing in his aunt's thick perfume. If only A'mmo Hakim could be alive again, tugging at his smooth white cuffs with the sparkling cuff links. Because of a stupid Sunni, he now lay in a white coffin, dressed in his white suit.

All over Iraq—even before the American soldiers had arrived—Sunnis and Shiites had been at war. Even though they were all Muslims, they found reasons to hate each other.

Up until now, Nouri hadn't felt any bad feelings toward Sunnis.

Now he thought of Baba's elder brother, who'd married a Sunni. They had a son his age—his cousin. Talib was half Sunni, half Shiite, but Nouri had never thought anything of it before. He and Talib had grown up happily together.

But now, when Nouri pictured Talib—his curly hair and narrow eyes—it seemed like a shadow passed over his cousin's image.

Because of a stupid Sunni, Nouri had had to ride to the cemetery in Najaf City in A'mmo's black car. And now Baba was about to sell that car, the last remains of Nouri's beloved uncle.

ALLAH IS GREAT

With a low, grinding sound, an American tank drove into the neighborhood. It filled the narrow street, scraping against a wall, crushing rocks as it moved. It stopped right in the middle of Talib's war game.

What luck, Talib thought, to have a real tank right here. The American tanks cruised into Karada every now and then, but it had been a while. The tanks traveled slowly and usually never hurt anyone. Talib eyed the dull green metal and the long treaded wheel that moved the tank forward.

"The infidels kill children," whispered his cousin Nouri, crouching. "They break down doors and kill whole families."

Talib shaded his eyes and studied the tank again.

"But sometimes they give out candy." He put down his gun and got up. With a chance to get close to an American vehicle of war, how could his cousin act so cowardly?

"But your mother . . ." Nouri glanced toward the house, his straight black hair swinging across his forehead.

Mama worried endlessly about nothing. "She'll be all right. We soldiers do what we have to do." Talib hopped over the wall and slid into the space between the wall and the tank. Today he felt as tough as the tank itself. He went up to it and banged on the metal side. He called out: "Hello, Mister!"

A few yards down the dusty street, Nouri clustered with their other cousins, Jalal and Anwar. Two years younger, they stood only as high as Nouri's shoulder. The three whispered together.

They always let him be the brave one, Talib thought.

There was no sign of life from the tank. "Hello, Mister!" Talib repeated more loudly. In spite of his bravado, his stomach tightened. Was Nouri right? Every week there were stories of American bombs hitting the wrong target, killing civilians. What were the soldiers inside the tank doing?

Just as Talib took a step back, a soldier poked his head out the small window. He had a round, sunburned face.

Talib waved and the soldier smiled.

"Candy! American candy!" Talib hollered up in English.

The soldier drew his head back inside. A moment later, he lowered a combat helmet down the side of the tank.

Talib stood on tiptoe. He jumped up to see, but the helmet was still too high.

The soldier laughed and dropped the helmet. It fell with a hard plunk. Two red cans of Coke rolled into the dust.

Talib scrambled to grab the cans. Soda—especially American soda—was a rare treat. He picked up the heavy helmet and put it on. He heard giggles from his cousins. With real army equipment like this, he'd be more of a real soldier. He looked up at the window, but the solider had retreated inside. Maybe he didn't care about the helmet. With the Cokes in his arms and the helmet on his head, Talib hopped back over the wall.

He heard the soldier calling after him. Although he couldn't understand the English, he knew the words were rough. Talib paused. Allah wouldn't approve of his taking the helmet. The soldier needed it for protection. But it would be too shameful to turn back now.

Talib crouched in the thorny bougainvillea, head down, the cans against his chest, the helmet low over his eyes. That soldier wouldn't dare get out of his tank. He peeked up to look at the big gun. What if it turned in his direction?

The other boys joined Talib in the shadow of the wall.

"That took guts," said Anwar. He eyed the helmet on Talib's head.

Glancing at the tank, Nouri reached out to touch the helmet.

"Are you going to share the Cokes?" Anwar pointed to the cans.

Talib adjusted the helmet to see better. "Should I?" he asked. "You didn't help me get them."

"You should share," said Jalal, looking at the others.

"Is that an order?" Talib asked, smiling.

"Yes," replied Jalal.

"If you don't share," said Nouri, "we won't play with you. After all, you're a Sunni."

Talib pressed the hard cans to his chest, his smile fading. "You know I'm not completely Sunni," he protested. "Only my mother is."

Anwar scooted closer to Nouri and Jalal saying, "You can't be Shiite if you're half Sunni."

"But Baba is a Shiite like you," Talib protested further. "He's your uncle."

Anwar shrugged.

With white bougainvillea flowers dropping like soft bombs, Talib's three cousins—his very blood— suddenly looked at him with the hard eyes of enemy soldiers. He'd been braver than all three of them put together, but now that meant nothing.

He knew that Nouri's uncle had just been killed by a Sunni bomb. But that hadn't been *his* fault.

Talib handed over one of the cans. "You three can share this. The other's mine."

Jalal popped the tab, and Talib popped his. The soda, shaken in the fall from the tank, shot out and sprayed them with warm, syrupy sweetness.

Anwar laughed, wiping his face with the hem of his shirt.

"What about the helmet?" asked Nouri. "We each want to try it on."

Talib hesitated before handing it over.

Just as Nouri was placing the helmet on his black hair, the muezzin called, ordering them to prayer— *Allah is great! There is no god but Allah!*

Talib didn't like the fact that it wasn't a real muezzin calling, that it was only a recording blasting from the tower. He pretended the call came from a real man, a man whose heart overflowed with the love of Allah, the way his own heart overflowed.

Talib drained the last of his Coke and tossed the can aside. Even though his cousins ignored the muezzin's call, he never missed prayers. In order to be pure for Allah, he needed to wash. But since there was no water, he'd have to use sand.

As he stood up and reached for a handful, he caught sight of Nouri looking out from under the helmet, still seated.

As Nouri passed the helmet to Jalal, Talib finished rubbing sand between his palms. But he couldn't pray with a clean heart without giving the helmet back.

Talib lifted the helmet off Jalal's head. He jumped over the wall. He hoped the soldier wouldn't shoot him. Laying the helmet below the window of the tank, he called, "Mister!"

Back on the other side of the wall, Talib turned in the direction of Mecca, knelt, then bowed forward, pressing his forehead to the dust. He sank into the earth: *Allah is great. There is no god but Allah.* . . . As he bowed down, everything vanished from his mind—the tank, the fight, his cousins. *Allah is great.* . . . Even the sun, the sky, the very ground vanished as Talib let Allah's sweet presence fill his being. Allah was as close as his own breath.

KERPOW YOURSELF

"Time to eat!" The voice of Nouri's mother sailed through the air.

Nouri led the way into the courtyard where A'mmo Hakim's car was parked. "Don't touch it!" he ordered his cousins, glaring at Talib.

Beyond the dry fountain, the smallest cousins sat on the flagstones making mud pies, their hands red with cold.

Nouri pushed open the door into the big room off the courtyard. The members of his Shiite family ate together every Sabbath. Inside were gathered A'mma Hiba, his aunt, and many more aunts, uncles, and cousins from all over the city. Because of A'mmo's death, they wore black.

Baba stood, his hands on his hips, talking with A'mmo Murtadha. Baba's face was red, as if he'd been arguing.

Nouri held the door wide for his cousins, but his grip tightened as Talib passed into the room. Talib wasn't really welcome. Not after the bombing.

Talib's mother was the only Sunni here, and Talib was the only person of mixed blood. They came only because A'mma Fatima had no relatives of her own in Baghdad.

They came without her husband and Talib's father, A'mmo Nazar. On the Friday Sabbath, when many liked to shop, Nouri's uncle tended his book-stall on Mutanabbi Street.

Mama stood near the table of food, her silver brace-lets clattering on her wrists. She directed the other women: place the dishes here and there, over there.

"Smells good," said Jalal.

"But it's not what she used to make," said Anwar.

Anwar was right. Before the war Mama would have served minced meat with nuts, raisins, and spices, and *quzi*, roasted and stuffed lamb. Now she offered less expensive dishes like *dolma*, tomatoes stuffed with rice. But at least there was always food since Baba had a good job as a security guard.

Before the war they'd all dug deep with the big serving spoons, piling the fragrant food on their plates, covering it from one edge to the other. But lately on these Fridays, there was only enough for everyone to take a little.

There wasn't really enough, Nouri thought, for Talib and A'mma Fatima.

Nouri spotted Talib's mama in a pink head scarf, black curls showing around the edges of her face. She was sitting with the small girl cousins. Usually she ate with Mama and Hiba and the other women, chatting and laughing. But today she sat, like a children's nanny, in the corner. That was where she belonged.

From behind him, Nouri couldn't help overhearing a conversation between Baba and two of his uncles.

"The Sunnis are working with the Americans now."

"Over in Anbar Province."

"First those Sunnis betray us with Hussein, and now they do a double cross and go over to the side of the occupiers."

"Instead of offering jobs and other bribes, the Americans should clean out that nest at Anbar . . ."

"Shhh," A'mmo Murtadha said, glancing at Talib's mama. Anbar province was the home of A'mma Fatima's Sunni family.

But Nouri found himself hoping that A'mma Fatima had heard. A Sunni had bombed the market where A'mmo Hakim had died. A Sunni like Talib and his mother. And Nouri felt they should pay.

Mama handed down a plate of cubes of braised lamb, saying, "Share this among yourselves."

Nouri took three pieces and passed the plate to Jalal and Anwar, who also took three. Only when there was one bite of lamb left did Nouri offer the plate to Talib.

After the meal, while the men smoked and talked, the women cleared the dishes, then spread out blankets and pillows for napping.

Nouri led the way to the large room where Mama kept her potted orange trees in winter, where sunshine spilled through the glass ceiling. Pigeons flew in through a broken pane, darting in the muted light.

"*Kerpow!*" Jalal shouted, making a pistol with his hand, his index finger pointed at Talib.

"Kerpow yourself," Talib retorted, standing motionless.

"Aren't you going to play?" asked Nouri. Although part of him wanted to play as they had all these years, pretending to be enemies, another part of him felt like it wasn't so much a game anymore.

"He's going to sleep like an old person," said Anwar, pillowing his head on his folded hands.

Nouri watched as Talib sat down on the cement floor and scratched patterns in the dust. When the twig broke Talib tore off another.

A mortar shell dropped somewhere in the city, the loud blast rattling the panes of the glass room.

In the orchard of potted orange trees, the smaller cousins began to play hide-and-go-seek, crouching beneath the glossy leaves, slipping behind a large dusty tapestry. They shrieked whenever someone was found.

"Let's play that too," said Anwar.

"That's a little kids' game," answered Nouri.

"What are you going to do then?" Jalal asked.

Nouri gestured toward his uncle's black car, covered in dust in the driveway. "Clean it."

"Can we help?" asked Anwar.

Nouri shook his head and walked away, leaving his cousins behind. He didn't want anyone else to touch his uncle's car.

Taking one of Mama's kitchen cloths, he wiped off the dust, his straight dark-brown hair, his round chin reflected in the black finish. Wiping, he noticed dings in the paint he'd never seen before, including a long scratch along the bottom of the passenger door.

He polished until the little black car mirrored the branches of the *nabog* tree arching overhead.

When Mama rang a tiny bell announcing afternoon tea and sesame cookies, Nouri noticed that Talib was no longer there. He wasn't in the orchard. Nor were he or his mama in the big room.

They'd taken the hint, Nouri decided.

NO BREAD TONIGHT

Talib led the way across the courtyard, past the tiny black car. He went out through the gate to the broken sidewalk.

"Thank you for rescuing me," Mama said as they walked toward home.

"I hoped that was what you wanted."

"I was so uncomfortable. . . ."

"They're upset about Nouri's uncle."

Mama tugged at her head scarf. "But that had nothing to do with us. . . ."

As they walked, Talib ran his fingertip along a wall of graffiti. At the far end, Saddam Hussein had been drawn with devil horns. Someone had thrown red paint across one side of his face.

"My cousins weren't friendly either," Talib mumbled. He still felt wounded by their words, words that had felt like the bougainvillea thorns that had scratched his hands during the game of war.

...

Mama cooked dinner while Talib did his mathematics homework at the kitchen table. The water had been shut off again and Mama dipped into the extra jug she kept in the corner for emergencies.

She wore a jacket since kerosene had become scarce. So much had changed with the war. Even though Talib had been very young when the fighting had started, he remembered the days when food had been plentiful, water ran freely from the taps, and the house had been bright with electric lights.

Mama tucked her head scarf around her neck. By the way she paused and listened, Talib sensed her waiting for Baba's approach.

Although his hands were stiff with cold, Talib penciled his fractions on crinkled yellow paper. He wrote very small in order to fit all the problems on the sheet that his teacher, al-Khaldoun, had allotted him.

He erased, and the paper tore.

Mama sucked in her breath.

In the upstairs apartment where the Korashi family lived, Talib heard loud words, footsteps running across the ceiling, then a door slamming. It seemed as though everyone was scared or angry lately.

Talib bit his lip. With each equation, he too began to listen for Baba's return.

He listened to mortar shells flying and bursting. The city was divided into zones: the main one was the Green Zone where the American and Iraqi government buildings were located, and the area just outside it was called the Red Zone. Talib lived farther out, beyond the Red Zone. Tonight shells crossed the Tigris River, shelling the Red and Green zones and sometimes, probably, areas beyond.

Just as Talib had finished the last column, he heard his father wipe his boots on the mat. The doorknob jiggled and Baba entered, his footsteps loud on the stone floor. He unwound a red scarf from around his shoulders and laid it over the back of a chair.

Then Baba reached into a bag. "For you," he said to Talib, placing a book on the table beside the page of numbers. "You'll like it."

"Thank you, Baba." Talib flipped through the pages of *Daoud the Camel Boy*. It looked all right. There were even ink drawings. But really, Talib thought, no book could ever be as exciting as playing outside. A page was just black words on white paper.

While Baba washed up, scooping water from the jug, Mama brought *yabsa*, white beans cooked with tomatoes, and a plate of eggplant to the table. "There's no bread tonight," she said. "The bakery shelves were empty."

"And I didn't sell a single book today," Baba said, drying his hands. He sat down to spoon *yabsa* onto his plate. "No one has money, but people still come. They love to browse. Reading is one of the only pleasures left to us in this city." He sighed.

Talib noticed Mama biting her bottom lip.

"But instead of *buying* books," Baba went on, "people are bringing their collections to sell to us booksellers. People don't need books when there's so little food."

Suddenly, Mama lifted her face, her cheekbones illuminated by the single bulb, saying, "Maysoon and Hiba have been avoiding me at the Friday gatherings. They don't make a place for me. In the kitchen, they don't talk to me. They say unkind things about Sunnis."

"It's true," said Talib.

Baba reached out to touch her shoulder. "I'll speak with them," he said. "You're my wife and they have no right . . ."

"The hate that's spreading everywhere has infected even them. . . ." Mama went on, a tear wandering down her face.

"I'm sorry, Fatima," said Baba, rubbing his thin cheeks with his hands. "Things are changing in confusing ways."

"I've decided not to go there anymore," said Mama.

"Me neither," said Talib, scooting his chair closer to Mama's.

Baba was silent, looking down at his lap.

Talib looked toward the window, black with night. Was his father angry with Mama? Was he angry with him?

But then Baba raised his face. "Next Friday, we can all go to Mutanabbi Street instead," he said. "We can pray at the mosque in Etafiea."

Mama shook her head. "I'd rather pray here in peace and quiet."

That didn't surprise Talib. Mama liked to roll fresh jasmine flowers into her prayer mat. In the afternoons, when Talib returned from school, he found the flowers strewn on the floor, the air infused with their sweet scent.

"When I hang the laundry," Mama went on, "Batool always used to hang hers at the same time, so we could chat. But today Batool didn't come outside to see me."

"Maybe she's ill," said Baba.

"No," Mama hesitated. "Later she and Adiba bought tangerines from the street vendor. When I came out, both of them pretended not to see me."

"Things are changing," Baba repeated.

Talib helped himself to the circles of eggplant like big soft coins. His arm felt heavy.

After dinner, Mama made a pot of spicy chai tea. When she took the tea glasses down from the shelf, her hands shook—as they always did these days—and the glasses clattered.

Talib went back to his numbers, working toward just one precise answer, pretending not to listen to Mama and Baba's talk of changing times.

"The Ibrahims are leaving." Baba lowered his voice. "Going to Syria."

Mama's eyes widened.

Talib's pencil hovered over his paper.

The Ibrahims were Sunnis. They owned a car and were always giving people rides in case of emergencies. Once they'd taken Nouri's Shiite grandmother to the hospital.

"A time may come. . . ." said Baba.

"We don't need to move away," Talib said, anticipating Baba's words. "While you're at Mutanabbi Street, Baba, I'll take care of Mama."

Baba smiled. "And when you're in school? Who will take care of her then?"

"Allah," Talib replied with a smile.

PIGEONS

As Nouri threw a stone at a flock of pigeons, Anwar and Jalal leaned down to gather more ammunition. The birds moved from the wall to the overhead wires, then to a rooftop.

Across the street, Talib picked up a rock and hurled it. The pigeons took off into the sky.

"Now they're gone," complained Nouri, calling to Talib. "You chased them off."

"They'll come back," said Talib.

"After we're gone," Anwar muttered.

"Mama and I aren't going to your stupid Friday gatherings anymore," said Talib angrily. Then he hurried off to school without them.

"Wait up, Talib!" shouted Jalal. "We don't care *that* much about the pigeons. . . ."

Nouri elbowed Jalal in the ribs, muttering, "*I* care." He took a small strip of cloth from his pocket and used it to flick a stone in Talib's direction.

. . .

The school was made up of a group of low brick buildings surrounded by walls. Rows of palm trees grew close by. A doorkeeper stood watch.

As Nouri joined the students milling about the courtyard in their blue and white uniforms, he overheard snatches of conversation: ". . . an American soldier shot a *blind* man . . ." ". . . my uncle's getting work as a policeman . . ." ". . . I danced all night at my brother's wedding."

When the hand bell was rung, Nouri went to his mathematics class. Jalal and Anwar, being two years younger, had different teachers. Nouri wished it were one of them and not Talib who was his age.

The teacher, al-Khaldoun, had appointed Nouri to be the *Moraqib*, the watcher of the class. Whenever anyone did anything wrong, Nouri told al-Khaldoun. But in spite of his offering this information, the teacher never gave him high mathematics marks.

Nouri watched Talib cross the cement floor of the classroom. He laid his yellowed sheet of figures on the teacher's desk.

Would al-Khaldoun, a good Shiite, be thinking of the bombing of the market? Might he refuse to accept Talib's homework?

When Talib took his seat, instead of putting his book satchel on the floor, he held it against his chest like a shield.

Nouri heard the sound of al-Khaldoun's shiny black shoes coming down the hallway. At the moment the teacher stood in the doorway, Nouri issued the command: "Stand up, class!"

With a clatter of chairs, everyone stood.

Al-Khaldoun signaled for them to sit down again, flashing a smile with his white teeth. He smiled, Nouri noticed, even at Talib.

Nouri stared at the dark rectangle on the wall where the portrait of Saddam Hussein had once hung. It was good that the dictator was gone, good that his stupid Sunni government had been taken out too.

But some said that at least the face of Hussein had been clear for all to see. The dangers had been known. Now the perils were shadowy, revealing themselves slowly. Who knew what strange alliances would form? Or whose uncle would be killed. Some dangers were still as blank as the rectangle left by Hussein's portrait.

So how could al-Khaldoun smile at Talib? A Sunni like Saddam.

After the lesson, Nouri approached al-Khaldoun. "Did you know, sir, that Talib Jassim isn't completely Shiite? Did you know his mother is Sunni?"

Al-Khaldoun nodded gravely. "I did know, Nouri. But thank you."

Nouri turned so quickly that his satchel almost slid off his shoulder. Al-Khaldoun should care. At the very least, he shouldn't reward a Sunni with smiles.

BASKETBALL

A basketball team was forming on the far end of the court. Nouri, as usual, was the captain. As Talib approached, Nouri whispered and nodded in his direction. The others drew in tighter.

Talib stopped. He turned to look at the opposing basketball team. It was a motley collection of Shiites and a few Sunnis like Salaam Abdullah with his thick glasses. It wasn't made up of family.

Talib had never played with those boys. He'd *always* sided with his cousins.

He walked toward Nouri's team. He wanted to stand in that circle with his cousins. He needed to be one of them, to be no different.

This time, when Anwar whispered, Jalal and Nouri laughed.

Talib put his hands in his pockets and looked at the sky, acting as though he didn't care. A breeze carried a swirl of leaves, papery bougainvillea petals, and candy wrappers across the court. He felt as though that little bit of wind blew right through him. As though he were becoming transparent.

Several girls, one wearing a head scarf, were studying at the tables. Maybe he should join them and begin his homework. If he came home with his Arabic lesson done, Mama would be happy.

But he wanted to feel the familiar dust of the basketball on his hands.

Talib moved toward his cousins.

They didn't say a thing but when the game started, no one passed Talib the ball. He darted back and forth at the sidelines feeling as though he'd been blown away after all, as though he wasn't really there.

THE GAME WHIZ

Nouri sat on the floor of the balcony, pressing his forehead against the railing. Mama and Baba were arguing in the courtyard below.

Baba had just gotten off work. He still wore his dark blue uniform with the wide belt cinching his waist tight.

"Last Friday you and your sisters were ignoring Fatima," Baba was saying. His hair was mussed, as if he'd been running his fingers through it.

Mama put her hands on her hips, yet turned away, her pale face reflected in the car's black surface. "What do you mean?" she asked. "Fatima chose to sit away from us."

"Don't pretend you don't know." Baba took Mama's arm and spun her around to face him.

Nouri pulled his jacket tighter. Even from this far away, he could see Mama's lower lip trembling.

"I like Fatima well enough, but things are changing, Mohammed," Mama said slowly. She tucked a bit of hair under her head scarf. "I'm afraid that we—our children—will no longer be safe if a Sunni is welcome in our home...."

Baba's voice grew louder. "This is my *brother's* wife. She must not be treated that way. To help heal matters between us, I will go with him to pray. And I shall take Nouri."

He stepped quickly across the flagstones, toward the door into the house.

At the sound of the door slamming, Nouri scrambled up. He listened for Baba's footsteps on the stairs.

Moments later, Baba stood in the doorway, his hair still rumpled. "I'm going to Buratha today, and you're coming with me," he announced.

"But I don't *want* to go," said Nouri. He'd miss Mama's Friday feast. The sesame cookies would be gone when he got back. He lifted his chin, saying, "Why are you being so nice to someone who went and married a Sunni? A'mma Fatima is probably related to Saddam Hussein or to the martyr who killed A'mmo Hakim."

Baba took two steps forward and slapped Nouri smartly on the cheek. "Don't you dare speak like that. That is my brother's family you're talking about."

Clenching his teeth, Nouri put his hand to his hot face. A'mmo Hakim would never have struck him.

…

Baba turned the key in the black car. The engine sputtered and died. Baba tried again and the car roared, shooting gray smoke from the tailpipe.

The air was so cold that Nouri could see his breath but the spot on his cheek still burned.

Baba banged the bumper against the gate as he reversed. As he pulled forward and backed up again, Nouri held his breath. *He* would never drive so carelessly.

When they arrived at the tiny market, closed due to the war, A'mmo Nazar and Talib rounded the corner.

Nouri noticed that, at their approach, Talib slowed his steps.

Baba rolled down the window and called out: "Nazar! Let me drive you to Buratha."

"A fine idea," called back A'mmo Nazar.

"Get out of the front seat," Baba said to Nouri, gesturing as if to flick a spot of lint from his coat.

A'mmo Nazar climbed in the front, while Talib got in the back with Nouri.

"We haven't prayed at Buratha in a long time," Baba said as he headed down the road.

They passed a picture of an American flag with a big red slash across it.

In the seat ahead, A'mmo and Baba began to talk in low tones. Nouri wanted to listen, but Talib kept talking.

"Look at the Tigris—it's so low," Talib chatted. "I wonder if the war is making it so low. What if it dries up?"

Meanwhile, Nouri overheard Baba ask A'mmo why Fatima had sent word to Maysoon that she wouldn't be attending the Friday gatherings. A'mmo Nazar was explaining that she felt unwelcome. He said there were new tensions.

Baba said that those tensions shouldn't interfere with *family* ties.

A'mmo countered that obviously the tensions had already interfered with the family. "Do you think that's the tank that came to your street the other day?" Talib pointed, drowning out Baba's response.

"I've counted eleven buildings with holes blown in them. And look!" They passed a blackened car with a pair of legs poking out from underneath.

"That's nothing," said Nouri. "I see that every day."

Men hawked newspapers by the side of the road. As the car idled at the traffic light, Nouri caught a headline: *Six Injured in Blast*

That was only fair, he thought to himself, after the bombing at the market. After the senseless death of A'mmo Hakim.

"See, Mohammed," said A'mmo, pointing out the window, "what happens in the city, happens in your home."

"Fatima has been imagining things."

Nouri wondered why Baba would say that. Baba himself had just berated Mama for treating A'mma Fatima badly.

Nouri shifted on the seat. If Baba found out that he'd been mean to Talib, he'd be angry.

When the tall minaret of the Buratha Mosque was visible out the window, Baba pulled into a parking spot, and shut off A'mmo's car.

PRAYERS AND BOOKS

Talib shaded his eyes with his hand and gazed up at the reddish stone building of the house of Allah, at the white dome like a gigantic half onion. He'd been coming here for as long as he could recall.

"It's not just a recording here," he said to Nouri as the muezzin called. "See—up there—a man in the minaret."

Two security guards stood at the entry to the courtyard. They looked over each person who came in, alert for martyrs. There was no way they could tell the difference between Sunnis and Shiites since they all looked alike.

In the cold courtyard shaded by the tall walls, Talib and Baba, Nouri and A'mmo lined up behind the other men and boys to use the water tap.

When it was Talib's turn, he washed his right hand, then his left. He poured water into his mouth, tipped back his head, and gargled so his voice would be clean for Allah. He washed his wrists, his forearms. He wiped water quickly over his face and head, then washed his ears, the better to hear Allah. Finally, he bathed his feet and ankles.

When he'd finished with the icy water, Talib pulled his coat cuffs down over his wrists. He stepped aside, giving Nouri his turn.

Inside the mosque, the walls were decorated with patterns made from verses of the Koran. Talib remembered how during his first trip to the mosque, Baba had lifted him close, pointing out the way the lines and swirls were made up of words, a language that danced.

Talib and the others joined the huge crowd of men and boys as they stood on the tiles patterned to resemble prayer mats. Facing the mihrab, the archway showing the direction of holy Mecca, he quieted his heart.

The prayers began.

Talib loved the way the huge group moved in unison. Everyone was approaching Allah together. And to each of them, Allah would come. Talib placed his hands behind his ears: *Allah is great....*

Even Nouri and his father were joining in. In those holy moments, it felt as though Nouri had never said mean things nor tried to exclude him.

Talib touched his forehead to the cold ground: *Glory to Allah....*

Along with Nouri and the others, he rose and bowed again.

Even though the stone mat was cold and his body was chilled from the washing, Talib felt the tenderness of Allah fill his belly like a warm, sweet drink. He was one with the great throng that bowed and prayed together. His spirit, buoyed up on the rhythm of chanted prayers, swelled into the high-ceilinged room. It ascended to the round dome where it circled and danced. The outlines of his body melted and he disappeared.

· · ·

"We'll be going back home," said A'mmo Mohammed outside the mosque. "*Someone* has to show up there today."

"Plenty of people will show up," said Baba. "Why don't you let Nouri come along with us? He and

Talib can have fun together on Mutanabbi Street."

Talib watched as Nouri ignored them and took out his Game Whiz, bringing the tiny screen close to his face. Of course his cousin didn't want to go to Mutanabbi Street. He wanted to go home, to eat and play war with the others.

But A'mmo Mohammed nodded in assent. "That's a good idea, Nazar."

A frown crossed Nouri's face.

As they waited for the bus to Mutanabbi Street, Nouri kept focused on his Game Whiz. Talib wished Nouri would let him play.

With a great squeal of brakes, the bus arrived. As they boarded, Talib noticed the driver run his eyes up and down each of them.

"He thinks we're martyrs," he whispered. "He thinks we have explosives underneath our coats."

Nouri unbuttoned his coat and held out his hands, showing the Game Whiz.

The driver's eyes lingered on the game. Then he nodded slightly and Nouri stepped past the Iraqi soldier who stood behind the driver, his big gun slung across his chest.

Baba used his handkerchief to clean the red seat before he sat down.

Talib sat in the seat behind him, Nouri next to him.

Nouri played the Game Whiz without looking up, without saying a word.

The bus stopped on Rashid Street by the stand selling grape juice. Baba, along with several others, pulled the wire that signaled the driver.

They followed Baba past the cafés, past the *chai khana* selling steaming glasses of hot sweet tea.

Baba turned onto Mutanabbi Street and led the way in and out of the crowds. Whenever he stopped to browse through other vendors' books, Talib peered over Nouri's shoulder. But when his shadow fell across the tiny screen, Nouri twisted away.

Someone played slow, sad music on a violin outside, hitting a wrong note at the height of the melody.

On Mutanabbi Street it hardly seemed as though a war was going on. Everyone got along here. People sat at outdoor cafés, chatting in the shade of bright umbrellas. And yet, Talib thought, he and Nouri weren't getting along. Being with Nouri felt like the screechy note of the violin.

On the sidewalks, vendors sold used books ranging from the ancient text of *Gilgamesh* to Webster's dictionaries. They pushed carts of books, hawking them to passersby. Men in turbans and women with their hair hidden under headscarves stood alongside college students with their backpacks, fingering the books, flipping through the pages and reading passages.

Neon lights flashed. Double-decker buses cruised. Talib jumped up to tap the fringes of the bright banners above his head that announced all sorts of things for sale.

"*Marhaba*, A'mmo," said Talib as a man whom he knew passed, pushing a cart loaded with books. Hamid wasn't really his uncle, but he addressed him with respect.

"This place has lost its dignity," remarked Baba, pointing out a stack of children's Japanese trading cards for sale. "Foolish stuff."

Talib caught Nouri's eye and mouthed the word "later."

But instead of smiling in agreement, Nouri turned his gaze to the sky.

"Look!" Baba exclaimed. He picked up an ancient-looking book. "You're not selling *this* are you, Suheil?" he asked the bookseller.

Suheil al-Hassan made a face. "I have to. For my family's sake."

"I wish I had the money to buy it," Baba said, his fingers caressing the old leather cover.

"*Marhaba*, Talib!" cried al-Nakash from his bookstall across the street, waving his fat little fingers at them.

Old issues of *Life*, *Newsweek*, and *Time* sat in neat stacks on the card tables in front of his stall, their pages brittle with age. They were magazines Talib loved to page through.

"*Marhaba*, A'mmo!" Talib responded. "I'll come back after I help Baba set up."

The small storeroom for Baba's books was located in the gap between two buildings. He unlocked the padlock and swung the plywood door open. Sunshine bathed the shelves.

Talib and Nouri helped Baba pull out the red carpet. Together they rolled the carpet onto the sidewalk, then unpacked the secondhand books from their boxes.

"This pile is for Arabic translations," Talib instructed Nouri. "Poetry goes here. Religion there. Books for kids in the front."

"Here's a good book," Baba said when the books were stacked in place. "Why don't you sit down for a while and read? I'll find another book for you, Nouri."

The cover of the book Baba handed him pictured a tall snowcapped mountain. In the foreground a boy Talib's age was beginning the climb, a backpack on his shoulders. Martyrs wore backpacks like that.

"It's an adventure story," said Baba.

Nouri reached for the book, but Talib shook his head at his cousin. He unwrapped his plaid scarf and laid it on an empty crate. "We're going to go see what's happening."

"Through books you can live many lives," Baba said, still holding out the book.

"One life is enough."

"Go on then," said Baba, sighing.

Talib stood up as an American fighter jet sped up, trailing a thin white cloud.

"They think they own our sky," said a woman in a checkered head scarf standing near their bookstall.

A man looked up from nearby, adding, "They do own our sky. Our streets. Even our homes."

"Without the Americans we'd be stuck with Saddam Hussein," the bookseller next door said.

"Ha!" the woman retorted. "At least we had peace under Saddam. Now look! Sunnis and Shiites are at each other's throats every day."

"The Americans are only after our oil," said the first man, putting the repair manual back on the stack.

This kind of talk confused Talib. He was anxious to be on his way. "I need to visit a friend," he said to Nouri, as they turned the corner.

"Where?"

"Upstairs over there." Talib pointed.

"I'll wait down here."

Talib narrowed his eyes. "Why? Is it because you think my friend is a Sunni?"

Nouri shrugged.

"Well, I'm not even sure if he is or not. But if you want to wait out here, go ahead."

Talib located the doorway between the teamaker's stove and the stand that sold silver bracelets. He climbed the dark stairs and rapped on the door three times with the heavy knocker. Sometimes al-Shatri didn't hear well.

"Come in!" a voice called out.

Talib opened the door to the familiar, dizzying smell of printer's ink.

"Ah, Talib," said Sayed al-Shatri from behind his worktable. "It's good to see you."

Talib stepped into the dusty room to greet his friend. Al-Shatri had untidy gray hair and wore gloves with the fingers cut off so his hands would stay warm, but his fingers could stay nimble. Al-Shatri printed the Arabic translations of works like Shakespeare's plays, the Bible, and, lately, computer manuals. The shop was filled with piles of paper, heaps of books, and the small wooden boxes that held the blocks of metal letters.

In one corner, Al-Shatri had a narrow bed. Once Talib had asked his friend why he didn't sleep in the small, mostly empty room that fronted on Mutanabbi Street.

Al-Shatri had laughed and said he liked to stay close to his work.

"Sit down," al-Shatri now said, waving a gloved hand at the tall stools. "I'll make tea."

As al-Shatri put a kettle on the small kerosene stove, Talib talked about how his cousins were treating him, how his aunts were treating Mama.

Al-Shatri nodded sympathetically throughout. When Talib had finished, the printer set down his glass and said, "My advice is to act as if nothing has happened."

Talib sipped from his glass of tea. He wasn't sure he could keep taking insults without fighting back.

"One of my cousins is down in the street waiting," he said. "He thinks you're a Sunni."

Al-Shatri smiled and reached for Talib's empty glass. "Don't keep him waiting any longer."

BURATHA

Nouri took the cellophane off a new pack of trading cards. He shuffled through the pictures of robotic creatures, when the bookseller said from behind him, "If you're not going to buy those, then move along."

"Well, I'm not going to by them *now*," said Nouri, tossing the cards down in a disorderly pile.

He strode away from the stall. Baba shouldn't have made him come to Mutanabbi Street. But what could he have said? If he'd defied Baba, his father might not have struck him right then, in front of A'mmo Nazar, but back in the cold courtyard, Baba would have yanked off his wide belt.

Even being here with Talib was better than another lashing.

Suddenly the ground rocked underfoot. Nouri looked back at the bookseller's table to see that the Japanese trading cards had all slipped to the ground.

Another bomb was shaking up someone's life. A few passersby stared at the sky. Most acted as if nothing had happened.

"That was a big explosion," Talib said from behind him.

"Well, yeah," Nouri answered. It didn't take a genius to know *that*. But in his mind, he was calculating where the bomb had fallen. It seemed to be quite close by, which meant everyone in faraway Karada would be safe as they enjoyed the Friday feast he was missing.

They wandered past the bookstalls, finally arriving at the stall of American magazines they had passed as they'd come in that morning.

Nouri made a face. "These are all *old*."

"But they're interesting. Look." Talib picked up one with pictures of the Vietnam War. "Baba says the Americans compare our war here with the Vietnam War. But look at the jungles! And these people don't look like us at all. How can it be the same?"

"It's because the war goes on and on without purpose," put in a teenager standing nearby counting money into a box. A faint mustache darkened his upper lip and a few straggly hairs sprouted on his cheeks. Nouri guessed he must be the owner's son.

"Cool tanks. Cool guns," said Nouri, interested in the magazines in spite of himself. He turned to a magazine with a photo of pretty, laughing Marilyn Monroe. "Look at her. She's pretty."

"The Americans love their wars," continued the teen.

Nouri looked at the boy more carefully, and noticed the outline of a pocketknife in his back pocket.

Just then a man ran along the street, crying out: "A mosque has been bombed!"

"Which mosque?" Nouri asked, worried despite himself.

In a matter of moments, a crowd had gathered in the street. Nouri worked his way to the center, pushing himself very close to the man who'd brought the news. The man's coat smelled of mothballs. In the distance, he heard sirens.

"The mosque in Etafiea."

Nouri's mind spun wildly.

"The *Shiite* mosque?" a woman asked.

"Buratha," the man nodded.

Nouri sucked in a breath. That was *his* mosque. His Shiite mosque. And now it was gone. The rumble of the earth had been the bomb striking the mosque. "A damned Sunni did it," he muttered, pushing back against Talib.

"Retaliation for yesterday's bombing," someone said.

Al-Nakash turned on a handheld radio and everyone hushed.

Nouri cupped his hands around his ears to hear better.

Coming from the radio, the sirens that had wailed in the distance now sounded even closer. The announcer's voice was hurried, as though the information was coming to him as fast as machine gun fire. "The martyr appears to have been a young boy. Evidently, he aroused no suspicion. He walked right in without anyone stopping him."

A young boy. Like Talib. Like his Sunni cousin who stood in his shadow.

"Numerous persons are injured," the announcer went on. "Two are dead."

At that moment three American helicopters *thwack-thwacked* their way across the sky. Nouri's brain churned with the loud noise.

He faced Talib and grabbed the collar of his cousin's coat. The anger that had started out as a simmer was beginning to boil over. "You Sunni! You scum!"

Talib tried to step back, but Nouri held him fast.

"I loved the mosque as much as you!" Talib protested, his face screwed up. "My baba took me there!"

"You didn't *really* love it! You wished you were praying at one of your mama's stinking mosques!" Nouri pushed himself out of the crowd and walked quickly down a side street, away from Mutanabbi Street, toward the bus that would carry him home.

NO SUNNIS ALLOWED

On the way to school, Talib walked ahead of his cousins, who were throwing rocks at pigeons again. The dusty sidewalk was littered with soda can tabs, shards of glass, and the rubber soles of someone's sandals.

"The Buratha Mosque was bombed," one of his cousins called to him.

Talib looked back to see Jalal, jutting his chin into the air. "I know," he called back, transferring his backpack from one shoulder to the other.

"Sunnis bombed it," said Nouri.

"*Your* people," added Anwar. His hands were full of small stones.

"Not mine," Talib argued. "No relatives of Mama's would have done that."

Buratha had been his mosque too.

"How do you know they didn't?"

"Maybe your Sunni, Saddam Hussein, did it!" Jalal called out.

Talib tossed a stone over his shoulder at Jalal and walked on, moving as fast as he could without running.

Standing beside the doorkeeper, framed in the gateway, stood al-Khaldoun. Perhaps the mathematics teacher would greet the students with some special news.

As Talib approached, al-Khaldoun locked eyes with his. With a gesture, he drew him in.

"I'm sorry to tell you this, Talib," he said. "No Sunnis are allowed in this school anymore. Not since the Buratha bombing."

Behind al-Khaldoun, Talib glimpsed the empty basketball court. "But I'm only half Sunni. . . ." he protested.

Al-Khaldoun shook his head slightly. "It's a security issue."

Talib's backpack slid off his shoulder. It hit the ground with a thud. What would he tell Mama?

"Don't leave your books here, Talib," al-Khaldoun said softly. "Keep up your studies."

Talib picked up the backpack. As he walked away, he looked back to see Nouri, Anwar, and Jalal walking along, arms linked, big smiles on their faces.

Talib wanted to hurl himself at his smiling cousins, to pound them with his fists. But as he clenched his hands together, he saw that Al-Khaldoun was also turning away Kazem al-Maleki and Kazem's little sister, Noor.

Around the corner, Talib found Salaam sitting by the brick wall. "He kicked you out too?"

Salaam nodded.

Looking closer, Talib saw that Salaam's eyes were red and swollen behind his thick glasses.

"I'm going home," said Salaam. "This stupid school doesn't matter anyway. Our family is leaving for Anbar."

"You're moving?" Talib asked. He'd known Salaam ever since their first day of school.

"Tomorrow. I should help pack. Last night someone threw a rock through our window."

The words hit Talib like the rock itself, knocking out his breath. A faraway bombing was one thing— an attack on one's home was another.

"I'm sorry," he finally managed.

The street vendor who sold sandwiches during their lunch hour was walking up the street to set up his stand.

With the events of the day, Talib already felt famished. "Let's split one," he said to Salaam, holding out his lunch money.

Salaam nodded and took out a handkerchief to clean his glasses.

"*A'nba* only," Talib told the vendor. He didn't have enough money for falafel or eggs or for one of the shiny cans of Pepsi sitting temptingly in a bucket of ice.

The man split open the thick bread, making a pocket. With a wooden spoon, he scooped in the pickled mango syrup.

"Better hurry to school," the vendor said, handing over the sandwich.

"Not us," said Talib.

"Sunnis aren't allowed there anymore," Salaam added.

The vendor made a face, then slapped at his cart with a damp rag, muttering a bad word.

. . .

At dinner, Baba said, "On the way to Mutanabbi Street, I went to Buratha. The bodies had been taken away. But there was blood everywhere."

Talib had noticed the dark brown splatters on Baba's pant legs. He gripped the edges of his chair, feeling as though another distant rumble was passing through the earth.

Mama passed a basket filled with large round sheets of bread.

Watching her ladle soup into the bowls, he hardly cared that she'd made his favorite dish—*pacha*, soup made of lamb's head. The fragrant smell did nothing to lift his spirits. "What's left of the mosque?" he asked Baba.

"Part of the dome crumbled. The minaret fell too. But most is intact."

When Baba handed him the basket of bread, Talib tore off a big piece. He held it for comfort, the warmth entering him. "What about the writing? What about the verses from the Koran?" he asked.

"The writing wasn't damaged."

"Praise be to Allah," said Talib and Mama in unison.

As Talib put a bit of bread in his mouth, he had a tiny doubt, a wondering so small it merely tickled: whose God *was* Allah? Whose side was he on? On the side of the Sunnis—the side of his relatives?

A Sunni, like his mother, had bombed Buratha. A Sunni like half of him.

Talib wondered if the Sunni martyr had gone straight to Paradise, as Allah promised. But that implied that Allah was happy that the mosque had been attacked. How could this be? Was Allah the God of only the Sunnis?

If so, where did that leave his Shiite cousins? Where did it leave Baba?

Talib swallowed the bite of bread. The tickle was expanding into a mass of questions.

If Allah loved the Sunnis, then why did he allow Sunni mosques to be destroyed? Why did he let Shiite martyrs kill Sunnis?

Was Allah on neither side? Did Allah just stand back and watch the destruction?

Talib didn't understand.

"I stopped to help clean up some of the rubble," Baba said. "Just for a short time. I'll go again tomorrow."

"Can I help too?" asked Talib.

Baba shook his head. "That's not work for a boy your age."

"I'm strong enough!" Talib protested.

Baba shook his head again. "It's not physical

strength I'm talking about. There are things you're too young to see."

Talib dipped his bread in the soup. Baba was wrong. He could handle it. So far he'd kept the secret of being kicked out of school, and of the Abdullah family's departure.

Mama turned on the radio and the announcer's voice filled the kitchen: "A mob of gunmen went on a rampage through a Sunni district, pulling people from their cars and homes and killing them. It seems this violence was to avenge the bombing of the Buratha Mosque on Friday. . . ."

Mama sighed. "We're lucky such things aren't happening here."

"Fatima," Baba glanced at Talib, then lowered his voice, "I'm afraid it *is*." He looked toward the kitchen window and dropped his voice still more. "The other day when I was walking home from the bus stop, I saw a group of Shiites at the door of the Abdullah home. My brother Murtadha was the one knocking on the door."

"The Abdullah family has left town," Talib said. "Gone to Anbar."

Mama sucked in her breath.

"A rock was thrown through their window."

Mama cried out, while Baba stared into his bowl of soup.

"And I can't go to school anymore," Talib added.

"Why not?" Mama asked in a small voice.

"Sunnis aren't allowed anymore."

Baba pounded the table with his fist, but lightly, so that Mama's dishes didn't rattle too much. "I'll go talk to them."

"It won't do any good. It's a security issue, my teacher said."

Mama laid a hand on Baba's arm. "Should *we* move to Anbar?" she asked.

"We can't. I need to be close to Mutanabbi Street," Baba replied. "Otherwise, I have no work."

Talib studied his fingertips through the hem of the white lace tablecloth. Things were changing too fast.

Even life under a dictator had been better than this.

Talib lifted his soup bowl and drank from it, choking down small pieces of lamb. If his cousins caught him thinking like that about Saddam Hussein, they'd call him a Sunni traitor.

If only things could be normal again. He felt an urge to run outside and summon his cousins for a game of war. He wanted to shout and jump with them, as if only the playing mattered. But nothing felt like just a game anymore.

ONE, TWO, THREE!

By the light of the half moon, Nouri spotted the figures of Jalal and Anwar. They were waiting for him by the abandoned candy store, as planned.

Ever since the bombing of Buratha, Nouri's heart had burned like a hot coal. He had never felt so on fire as now, as he thought about what he was about to do.

The bombing of Buratha brought him closer to the bombing that had killed A'mmo Hakim. It made him feel closer to A'mmo himself. Had he been reaching for his favorite fruit—shiny tangerines—when the bicycle loaded with explosives went off? Had he died instantly, or had he suffered? Had A'mmo been carried on a stretcher like those Nouri had seen on television?

Carefully, he'd selected the rock—big enough to do the job, but not too big to throw. He'd written the note and wrapped it around the rock. The paper was damp from his sweaty hands.

When he reached his cousins, Jalal was whispering to Anwar, "Just think of it like throwing a stone at a pigeon. It's no different."

"But what if we get caught?" Anwar whispered back at him.

"We won't," Nouri said, without bothering to lower his voice. Maybe these two were too young after all. Maybe he shouldn't have invited them along.

He led his cousins through the shadows, avoiding the glare of the moonlight. Once they were startled by a cat jumping down from a wall, scattering loose stones.

At last they arrived at Talib's low wall. Anwar made a foothold with his clasped hands and Nouri stepped up.

Jalal danced back and forth.

"Stop that!" Nouri ordered, his voice a hiss.

No light was on in the house. Nouri found Talib's bedroom window glittering in the moonlight.

Anwar groaned and shifted his hands.

One, Two, Three! Nouri chanted to himself. Then he hurled the rock.

It traveled in slow motion, the white paper catching the moonlight. The rock traveled in a slight arc—traveling in memory of A'mmo Hakim—before smashing into its target.

At the sound of the shattering, Anwar released his grip and Nouri fell to the ground.

THE FIRST WARNING

CRASH!

The noise split the night. As Talib sat up, he heard a tinkling sound. When he touched his blanket, his hand met cold shards of glass. His heart pounded like a basketball.

He heard the sound of running footsteps.

Mama, then Baba, ran to the doorway. Baba flipped the light switch out of habit, but there was no electricity at night anymore.

"Don't move, Talib!" Mama shouted. "There's glass everywhere!"

Cold air drifted through the hole, along with a flood of moonlight. Talib stared into the white-lit room until he spotted the rock.

"Don't step on the glass," warned Baba. "I'll put on shoes and sweep it up."

Waiting, Talib looked closer at the rock. He noticed that it had a piece of paper wrapped around it. He jerked back the covers, and in spite of Mama's wails and the glass cutting his feet, marched over to the rock. He reached for it, removed the sheet of paper, and, by moonlight, read,

هذا انذاري الاول
[This is the first warning].

Baba returned in his shoes, and the three of them stood in the white light of the moon, reading and re-reading the words.

Mama began to cry softly. Baba said a bad word.

Talib threw the note down. He meant to cast it far away. But instead, the paper just lazily floated to his feet.

Baba swept the room, chasing the glass into a corner, muttering more bad words.

Mama led Talib to the bathroom, the only room without windows.

She lit an oil lamp and as the flame sputtered, she tweezed the glass from Talib's feet.

While she bandaged his cuts, Talib, guts twisting, tried to remember what his cousins' handwriting looked like.

...

A fierce sandstorm blew in from the desert and for days, everyone stayed locked inside. The sky grew as brown as a glass of tea. Sand seeped into the cracks, covering everything with grit. The wind howled like a battle cry.

Sand blasted through Talib's broken window even though Baba covered it with a piece of cardboard and taped it tight. Talib started sleeping on the floor of his parents' room.

He felt as though the sand was hitting his heart, chafing it.

...

In their isolation, Talib read Baba's book about the boy climbing a mountain. The boy was seeking treasure. Reading by the light of the kerosene lamp, Talib took turns imagining himself at the dark mouth of a mountain cave and looking hopelessly out at the relentless blast of sand. The entire desert was hurtling itself against their windows.

Mama set down a glass of tea for Baba. Wiping her hands on her apron, she joined him at the kitchen table. She rested her chin in her hands and said, "We can't keep living in this neighborhood, Nazar. Talib can't even go to school anymore."

Talib glanced up to see Mama's face partly lit by the lamp and partly shadowed by the darkness of the kitchen. He slipped a piece of paper in the page of his book. Without school, he wasn't sure it mattered if he read or not.

"Yes," agreed Baba. "Rocks thrown through windows is one thing. Next time it could be a bomb."

"What shall we do? What will become of us?" Mama pushed back her head scarf, running her fingers through her long curls.

"Oh, Fatima." Baba sighed. He pushed his glass of tea across the table. "Here, *you* drink this."

Mama shook her head.

"Maybe we could move in with your relatives," said Baba.

"That's too far from Mutanabbi Street," Mama said, echoing Baba's earlier words. "Besides," Mama looked at the floor, "as a Shiite, you might not be welcome."

Talib set aside his book. As half Shiite, *he* wouldn't be welcome either.

...

Because of the storm, there was no fresh food. And since mice had found a way into Mama's emergency stash of lentils, all meals consisted of dry bread and dates.

The muezzin's recorded call came through the cry of the storm, punctuating the days with the five sessions of prayer. Because the sand had blasted the jasmine off Mama's bush, she had no more flowers for her mat. But she still heeded the prayer call with Talib. Even Baba, who didn't usually pray, joined them as they faced Mecca.

Praying, Talib's mind wandered. For as long as he could remember, Talib had measured his days by the muezzin's call. No matter what came in between the times of prayer, he'd sunk effortlessly into the vast oneness.

So why had his merciful Allah let the rock fly through the window? And why *his* window when he joined Allah five times a day without fail?

He prayed that Allah would drain the well of bitterness from his heart. But questions buzzed like summer flies around his head.

. . .

They couldn't stay in their home, but where could they go? On the third day, shut inside their little apartment, Talib had an idea. He and Baba were sitting at the table, mending books. Placing a piece of tape across a torn page, Talib asked, "What about al-Shatri's printing shop? He has an extra room."

Baba looked at Talib, then back at the spine of a volume of poetry. He nodded slowly. "Mutanabbi Street is a neutral area. Shiites and Sunnis get along there. As soon as this sandstorm is over, you and I will go to al-Shatri and ask."

. . .

Sometime in the night the roar finally quieted. By morning, Talib looked out to see a bloodred sky.

"Keep the door locked, Mama," advised Talib as he and Baba prepared to leave.

"And you two get to the bus stop quickly," Mama responded.

"Look!" said Talib, pointing to a large black X painted on their door. He touched the glossy spray paint, the X gritty with red sand. Had someone come during the sandstorm? Or had someone painted this on the night the rock was thrown? Had the X been marking their house—and them—all these days?

Yellow leaves had been knocked off the trees. Trash littered the streets and sand was piled up against the walls. But it felt good to be out in the sunshine at last.

When the bus arrived, the brakes screeched so loudly that Talib plugged his ears.

Passing the mosque, Talib peeked in spite of himself. He saw the broken white onion dome. The once magnificent minaret had been reduced to a stub.

At Rashid Street they got off and Talib walked by Baba's side as he turned onto Mutanabbi. They passed the plywood that covered Baba's shelves of books, but Baba didn't stop.

Talib led the way between the tea maker and the seller of silver bracelets. Thick cold lurked in the dark stairway to al-Shatri's.

At the top of the stairs, Talib rapped with the knocker. He pressed his ear to the door, listening for his friend's footsteps.

Al-Shatri opened the door, his unruly gray hair tucked under a wool cap. "Why, Talib! And Nazar," he nodded to Baba, "what brings you here?"

Baba stood a little taller, then cleared his throat. "We have a request to make of you." He fingered the fringe on his red scarf.

"A request!" said al-Shatri, opening the door wider. "Before I hear your request, let's drink tea together." The printer brought three stools close to the kerosene stove. "That was a nasty sandstorm, no?"

Talib scooted his stool closer. The tiny flame of the stove looked warm.

Soon they each held a glass of hot tea.

When the glasses were empty and fresh tea poured, Talib told al-Shatri about the rock and its warning.

Al-Shatri arched his gray eyebrows.

"You heard, I'm sure," said Baba, "about what the Shiite militias did in that neighborhood."

Al-Shatri nodded. "It'll just bring more retaliation."

Baba twisted his glass between his big hands. "My wife and I worry that such violence could come to Karada as well."

"That could be true," said al-Shatri. He lifted his tea to his lips, his hand shaking slightly.

Talib couldn't stand the suspense. Baba was taking too long to ask! "Can we come live with you?" he burst out. "In your little room?" He gestured toward the closed doorway. "I can help you with the printing. With no school, I'll have time."

Al-Shatri looked at Talib, at Baba, at the closed door, then back at Talib. He wrinkled his forehead and smiled. "Yes, why of course. Anything for friends in need."

DRIED LENTILS

Wrapped in their wool head scarves, Mama and A'mma Hiba sat on the patio, picking the rocks out of a bowl of dried lentils.

Nouri sat behind the wheel of A'mmo Hakim's black car. He'd opened the window a crack so the glass wouldn't fog up with his breath. Earlier, he'd dusted off the red grime of the sandstorm. Soon he'd get a rag and clean out the sand that had gotten inside.

"Nazar's family is leaving," said Mama, pinching something out of the lentils with her long red fingernail.

Slowly, Nouri rolled the window all the way down.

He held himself motionless, listening, the vinyl seat smooth at his back.

"Maybe they'll go to Syria. Lots of people do."

"My husband's relatives went there."

"But Syria is a long way...."

The lentils clattered gently in the pot. A tiny stone bounced across the courtyard.

Nouri gripped the steering wheel tighter. Was Talib's family really leaving? He'd just wanted to scare his cousin, make him uncomfortable. He hadn't really thought he'd drive them away.

If Baba knew that his brother's family was going away because of *him*, what might Baba do?

Nouri shuddered.

"We should say good-bye," said A'mma Hiba.

"But others will see us doing so. We might be in danger," Mama whispered.

"What about the friendship between the boys?" A'mma's voice rose into the cold afternoon.

Mama sighed.

With his fingertip, Nouri drew two stick figures on the dusty dashboard. One had Talib's curls, the other had his own straight hair. He drew the figures close together. What had he done?

A SMALL WAVE

Dusty sunshine washed over Talib as he opened the door. The cold air smelled of gunpowder, vehicle exhaust, and Mama's bush of jasmine flowers. The fronds of the blue-green palms were stiff against the sky.

An engine idled while a taxi driver leaned against the fender, smoking cigarette after cigarette, his arms crossed.

Mama had packed up the bedding, clothes, a few dishes, and Talib's schoolbooks. She'd boxed up Baba's rare books, and the photographs of Talib's grandparents. Into her purse, she tucked the pearl necklace and cuff links that she and Baba had worn at their wedding.

As Talib carried bundles to the taxi, anger pounded through him. The home he'd always lived in was being torn apart. So much had to be left behind: Mama's pretty tea glasses that he'd closed his fingers around so many times, his bed with the horse carved into the headboard, the chessboard and its heavy marble pieces.

When Talib picked up his gun made from the whittled branch, Baba said, "You can't take that."

"Let him have it, Nazar," said Mama. "He's losing so much."

Talib saw Mama's friend, Batool, watching from the window. He saw old al-Marzooq with his bushy white hair. He turned around to see Malik al-Korashi who lived above them. These people had been neighbors for years, but none came out to say good-bye. None even waved.

Furthermore, there was no sign of Baba's relatives. The night before, Baba had gone to A'mma Maysoon's house. When he'd returned, he'd kicked the door closed.

"What happened?" Mama had asked.

"I gave them formal notice that we were leaving."

"And?"

"They said it was better that way."

"Better?" Mama's voice was high. "Better to be cast out into the *city*?"

"I think they meant they couldn't protect you and Talib if trouble comes."

Now the taxi was full. Baba closed the big padlock on the front door with the black X across it.

"We'll come back someday, won't we?" Talib asked Baba.

Baba stared at him for a moment, then patted his shoulder. "Of course we will."

Talib took a last look at the two-story tan building with the blue trim, the narrow gate.

Walking to the taxi, Mama kept her eyes on the ground.

The taxi driver threw the remains of his cigarette into the gutter and everyone climbed in.

As the taxi drove down the familiar streets, Talib pressed his face to the window glass.

Questions filled his head like the rat-a-tat-tat of gunfire: was he passing though Karada for the last time? Would he see the peddler again with his load of persimmons? Would he ever again take the path through the vacant lot littered with broken glass and bullet casings, his shortcut to school?

They drove past another door with an X painted on it. Like the one on his own door. It was the home of Zaid al-Najeeb, the Sunni auto mechanic.

Just then, by the side of the road, Talib saw Nouri. His cousin lifted his hand in a small wave.

Talib turned his face away.

...

"Welcome, my family," al-Shatri said in greeting. He shook the broom he was holding. "I just finished sweeping your new home." He opened the door to the empty room.

With five large footsteps, Talib crossed to the window overlooking Mutanabbi Street. Mama made beds on the floor while Baba stacked the dishes in neat piles. Talib laid his wooden gun next to his books. The room was so cold that with each exhale, a puff of steam bloomed from his lips. Who knew how long this would be home?

SWEET WHITE BERRIES

Nouri ran after the taxi until it rounded the corner, a small cloud of dust trailing behind. Maybe Talib and his family were taking the taxi to the transit station where buses left for Syria.

Would Baba learn why?

As Nouri walked home past a wall of graffiti, uninvited memories flowed through him. He recalled the days of eating *dolma* and Turkish delight with Talib. In summer, when the *nabog* tree was loaded with berries, he'd climbed the ladder to the roof with Talib. Perched precariously, they had feasted on the creamy white sweetness of the *nabog* fruit.

Would he ever do that with anyone again?

Just a few months ago A'mma Fatima had given Talib a birthday party, inviting many relatives, including Jalal and Anwar. She'd gotten a cake from the bakery, his name written in blue frosting. With the candles glowing, they'd all sung *Sana Helwa Ya Jameal*, Happy Birthday, Handsome!

It had not been that long ago. But now they'd never gather like that again.

JABIR

"As times grow hard, this place is turning into a flea market," Baba complained as he led the way down Mutanabbi Street. "Just look at the Winnie-the-Pooh stickers, those postcards of the London Bridge, those cheap pencils! Aren't books enough?"

Talib smiled, secretly liking those things.

Baba continued on to the bookstall, threading his way in and out of the crowd of people, commenting as he went: "And look at my friend Suheil. Now that his rare books are gone, he's having to peddle packs of chewing gum."

Besides the items that Baba complained about, Iraqis were selling prized collections of antique books, lamps, jewelry, and even furniture. As Talib and his father walked between the stalls with everything laid out on the street—looking a little shabby—he kicked at stones, skittering them down the street.

When his family went home again, would all their things be just as they'd left them? Was someone right now selling their household goods on a street somewhere?

Talib peeked into the famous old Shabandar Café where shadows spun around and around as the ceiling fans turned. Shadows passed over the black-and-white photographs on the brick walls. One showed Iraq's first king as a young man, while others boasted ancient buildings constructed during the Ottoman Empire. At a nearby table, a group of men in worn jackets sipped tiny glasses of sweet tea and debated the war.

Baba unlocked the storage shed and together they laid the books on the red carpet. After Baba was settled on a small stool, Talib wandered over to al-Nakash's stall to flip through the magazines.

"So you've become a resident, Talib," al-Nakash remarked.

"Just until the war is over. Then I'll go home."

"So you think the Sunnis and Shiites will be able to live together peacefully again one day?"

At first, Talib didn't answer. That was the big, hard question. Would his cousins every really accept him again? Could he forgive them? Would he ever feel safe in Karada again?

Then he had a new thought. He lifted his head. "But of course, A'mmo. Baba and Mama live together every day."

Al-Nakash chuckled and moved on to help a customer.

Sensing someone at his elbow, Talib looked to see al-Nakash's son, Jabir.

Casting his shadow across Talib, Jabir said in a low voice, "I heard you had to leave your home. That your own relatives made you go."

"Yes," Talib admitted. The news had spread quickly.

"Things like that shouldn't happen," Jabir murmured.

Talib shrugged. "Nothing I can do about it."

"Allah takes care of those who help themselves," said Jabir.

· · ·

While many stopped to look through the books spread on the red carpet of Baba's bookstall, few bought. When they did, they dropped the coins hesitantly into Baba's palm.

Fridays could be busy, but during the other days of the week, time passed slowly. Talib's mind turned to memories of home: the spicy smells of Mama's cooking, her kitchen floor strewn with onion peels and coriander stems, the persimmon tree brushing against the windows.

Someday all that would be his again.

To distract himself from such memories, Talib looked through Baba's books. He carried armfuls of books upstairs to read by the kerosene lamp. He read about golden fish that were really young women, about pomegranate trees and beautiful moons. He read about Rejab, the baby boy who lived with no food after his mother died. He found himself interested, and then captivated. Baba was right—through books he lived many lives. And right then, he preferred any life but his own.

While Baba focused on selling books, Mama wrote long letters to her relatives in Anbar Province, the paper rustling, her pen marching across the page.

Whenever the muezzin summoned the faithful to prayer, Talib bowed down. Yet Allah's sweetness began getting harder to find. He'd once daydreamed about the light that was Allah—the stars, the galaxies, the white body of the moon. But now when he tried to focus on Allah, only blackness greeted him.

In order to repay al-Shatri's hospitality, Talib ran errands for him on Mutanabbi Street and around the corner on Rashid Street, buying ink, onions, bags of lentils, and packets of tea.

In the late afternoons, Talib helped al-Shatri in the press. He sorted metal letters and boxed up books.

As they worked, al-Shatri played the radio. The announcers talked of little but war—conflict in Baghdad, Basra, and Mosul. The numbers of American troops were increasing. Bombs continued to fall in the Red Zone, and even around the edges of the Green Zone. Violence flared in the neighborhoods where Shiites and Sunnis lived together.

"Everyone is desperate," said al-Shatri as Talib set the kettle on the little kerosene stove, "and we Iraqis are beginning to lose our humanity."

Talib stared at the tiny stove flame. By hating his cousins, he himself was losing his humanity. He wished he could talk about his feelings with al-Shatri as he had before the rock had come crashing through his window. But his anger had grown so much stronger since then, he didn't dare speak.

...

Every time Talib went to the stall of al-Nakash, he looked for Jabir. Lately it felt like only Jabir understood him.

He and Jabir flipped through magazines together. In a voice like dried leaves blown along the pavement, Jabir commented on the photographs. On the assassination of the American president, JFK, he said, "Here in Iraq leaders get assassinated all the time and no one makes them saints." He dismissed the Beatles as tools of American imperialism. When Talib pointed out that they were English, Jabir swatted at the air, declaring, "Same thing."

Talib recognized Jabir's undercurrent of anger as his own. Hearing the teen's rough talk both exhilarated and scared him.

One day when the wintry wind blew, when Talib was idly scanning pictures of the Beatles' famous trip to the United States, he heard Jabir's voice at his shoulder. "It's time to get back at whoever made you leave your home."

Talib stared at a picture of girl fans screaming at the Beatles as though they were in the presence of Allah himself. A shiver ran through him.

"If you don't stand up for yourself, it will happen again."

Talib shrugged, hiding the way Jabir's words made every bit of him wake up and listen.

"Don't be a mouse."

BAKLAVA

Nouri carried baklava down Mutanabbi Street. Wrapped in newspaper, the flaky dessert that Mama had made that morning leaked honey onto the black words.

In Karada, bands of men and boys from all over the city roved, accosting any Sunnis who had the guts to show themselves in public. And when there were none, they knocked on doors, looking for the ones hiding inside. They dragged people from their houses and beat them up. Sometimes they forced them to board buses that would dump them at the outskirts of Baghdad.

Nouri often came upon a lingering smell of spray paint after someone had sprayed a black X on the door of a Sunni house or painted graffiti on a wall. The one by his house shouted: OUT ALL SUNNI DOGS! alongside crudely drawn pictures of Saddam Hussein.

The only Sunni left in the neighborhood was Zaid al-Najeeb. In his garage he fixed cars, never asking his customers to which sect they belonged. Every morning al-Najeeb came out to the street, placed his hands on his hips, and declared: "My father built this house. I will never leave it, even if I have to die!"

Mama forbade Nouri to go out at night now. "Because A'mmo Nazar is married to a Sunni, our family might become a target. That man in Mansour was executed because of his Sunni wife. Even though A'mmo Nazar's family is gone, people still remember. . . ."

But sometimes Nouri snuck out to meet Jalal and Anwar anyway, slipping into the night that was lit up by tracer fire. Instead of playing war now, they pretended to kick the Sunnis out of their neighborhood. They carried rifles made of branches, and took turns being the hated Sunnis. Whenever a mortar shell exploded, they pretended it was their guns that had fired.

Nouri half hated the game. Anwar and Jalal suddenly seemed so young, so unaware.

"Remember the night at Talib's?" Anwar asked every now and then.

Nouri wanted to forget that night. He wondered where Talib was, how he was doing. The little thing they had done had turned into a tidal wave of violence.

That morning, carrying his packet of baklava, Nouri wanted to find Talib. He wanted to make up with his cousin. He hoped that this little square of sweetness would help.

Nouri searched the stalls. Being Friday, the street was busy with men wheeling carts of books, idle shoppers, and vendors hawking their wares.

He found Talib standing behind a book display. He was smiling at a customer.

"Talib!" Nouri called.

Talib looked his way, and his smile faded.

"I brought you some of Mama's baklava."

Talib thrust his hands in the pockets of his too-short pants, saying, "I don't need sweets."

It wasn't like Talib to turn down baklava. Nouri wondered if he suspected him of throwing the rock that night. But if he did, he wouldn't be speaking to him at all. "You live here?" He looked around, clutching the packet.

Without a word, Talib indicated the second story of a nearby building.

"Isn't that the same building where you visited your friend?"

Talib nodded. He leaned down to straighten the fringe of the red carpet, saying, "What's going on at home . . . I mean, in Karada?"

Nouri hardly wanted to tell. Instead he wished he could bite into the baklava himself. "Someone broke into your house. They took your refrigerator." He didn't mention the destruction—the spray-painted walls, the way the furniture had been hacked to pieces, including Talib's bed with the galloping horse.

"How do you know?"

"I went in to look. . . ." He'd been accompanied by Anwar and Jalal, and they'd entered the house laughing.

"*You went inside our house?*" Talib's voice grew louder.

"Why not? I've been in there plenty of times."

"How did you get in?"

"All the windows are shattered."

Talib fisted his hands inside his pockets.

"Other Sunni homes," continued Nouri, "—those of the Ibrahims, the Zaydans, the Bassems—have also been vandalized." He wanted Talib to understand that his family hadn't been the only one. And he, Nouri, had had nothing to do with the leaving of those families, had not thrown any rocks through their windows.

"The new vandals are terrible," he went on. "They're Shiites who don't even live in Karada. Most carry guns, but some have rocks and even," he swallowed hard, "grenades."

Talib squatted to straighten a pile of books.

Guilt like a curtain of gray smoke passed over Nouri. He knew he was no better than those men. He, too, had been a vandal. "I'm sorry I got angry about Buratha that day."

Talib shrugged.

Nouri unwrapped the baklava, honey sticky on his fingers, and held it out.

Talib shook his head. But only slightly.

Nouri continued to hold it out to his cousin.

At last, to his relief, Talib reached for the sticky packet.

SPRING

GET DOWN!

That March morning Talib came to the bookstall wearing his winter jacket. By mid-morning, he took it off as a spring breeze blew in. Talib daydreamed of riding a camel, ambling over the sand dunes, rocking from side to side with the camel's heavy footsteps.

Just before noon prayers, a red two-story bus loaded with people edged through the traffic. A man wheeled a cart of books from one stall to another. A holy man wearing a turban strolled by.

A woman Mama's age, smelling of spicy perfume, requested a book of poetry by Hafiz. Talib knelt to look through a box, setting books on the carpet. He was giving the small red volume book to the woman when he was rocked off balance and the book fell out of his hand.

His whole world shifted. And then: rocking.

Falling.

Everything crashing.

Burning.

Screams.

Falling.

Collapsing.

"Talib!" Baba cried. "Talib!"

"Baba!" His voice was barely a whisper.

The woman ran, perfume trailing after her.

The world flashed red.

Glass exploded.

Fires leapt up.

"A car bomb!" someone shouted.

Car bomb. Here? On Mutanabbi Street?

Boom! Boom! Bang. Clatter, clatter, clatter.

Cries here and there.

Sirens coming closer.

Heart slamming.

Smoke.

Talib coughed.

"Run!"

The red book of Hafiz lay on the ground, black now. Crumbled.

"Baba!"

A groan. Baba on his side. Head in his hands red with blood.

"*Get down!*"

"*Get up!*"

"Nazar! Talib!"

"Here, Mama!"

"Praise be to Allah!"

"Baba's hurt!" said Talib, but Mama was there. Wiping blood with her dress.

Talib stood.

Baba's storeroom had been blown apart. Everything was black. The smell burned Talib's nostrils. The books were on fire all around him.

Down the street, Talib saw a huge empty space. The Shabandar Café was gone. In its place was the blue sky.

Everywhere Talib looked he saw ambulances, stretchers, and bodies. Groans and shrieks rose from all directions.

Fire trucks screamed down the street, spraying streams of water onto the smoldering mounds.

Over everything, Talib heard the muezzin calling— *Allah is great! Allah is great! There is no God but Allah!*

ANSWER ME!

After school, Nouri and Jalal dribbled and shot bas-
kets with a ball they'd found. It was slightly deflated
but they still managed to play.

Jalal had just passed the ball, and Nouri had
caught it, when a girl named Farrah, her head scarf
flying, came running. "Mutanabbi Street has been
bombed! Many people are dead!"

"Mutanabbi Street?" Nouri called back. "Are you
sure?" Such a thing couldn't happen on *Mutanabbi
Street*. Mutanabbi was a safe place. Everyone got
along there. People didn't care about which sect you
belonged to. Why would anyone bomb Mutanabbi
Street? His mind raced.

"Yes! It was a car bomb!"

Nouri held the basketball tight against his chest. What had happened to Talib? Was he safe? Nouri hadn't seen his cousin since he'd taken him the baklava a couple of months ago.

. . .

After school, Nouri boarded the bus. He'd told Jalal and Anwar that he had to help Mama clean their courtyard. And he'd told Mama that he was going to Anwar's to study for a geography test.

The bus was filled with others anxious to learn the fates of their loved ones.

"She went to buy a manual for her new computer. . . ."

"My son's stall is a landmark on Mutanabbi Street. . . ."

A young woman sobbed.

As the bus approached the street, smoky air leaked into the bus. Women drew their head scarves over their faces.

Just before Rashid Street, the driver stopped. Everyone flooded out the doors, some of them pushing.

"Go on! Hurry it up!" one man kept exclaiming.

Nouri ran down the street with those at the front of the crowd. Helicopters crisscrossed the sky and the afternoon was alive with the screams of sirens.

He slowed at the sight of people being stopped by Iraqi soldiers. No one was being allowed in! He scanned the street and, noticing a small alley, he ran down it, and climbed through a ruined building.

Finally he found himself on Mutanabbi Street.

Or on what was left of it.

Instead of the red two-story buses, American tanks idled at the curbs. American soldiers in green camouflage talked with Iraqi police, both sides writing in tiny notebooks, both sides speaking into walkie-talkies.

Nouri passed a blackened body covered with cardboard and pink stationery. The paper read: "The remains of Rahim. Hummus Seller."

"Keep digging!" a man shouted at two others, holding a black shoe. "This is my son's!"

When Nouri went by another shouting, "Answer me, Sanaa! Answer me!," he called out, "Answer me, Talib! Where are you? T-a-l-i-b!"

His heart pounded. It was all his fault that his cousin was here and not home in the first place! If Talib lay injured, or even dead, it was because of him.

As he tore through the wreckage, Nouri hardly recognized anything, much less the second-story apartment Talib had once pointed out. He tried one stairway after another, knocking on the doors. Sometimes there was no answer; sometimes a stranger appeared.

Finally, he found a pale blue door that seemed familiar. He knocked but no one came. He knocked again and was turning to leave when someone drew back the bolt.

The door opened to reveal A'mma Fatima. She was pale, her cheeks smudged with ash. "Why, Nouri . . ."

"*Marhaba*, A'mma. You're okay! I came to see Talib. To see if he's all right. . . ."

"Come in, then." She led him through a room where an old man sat on a stool sipping tea, and then into a smaller one where A'mmo Nazar lay on a bed on the floor, his head bandaged.

"*Marhaba*, A'mmo. I'm sorry for your injury." Nouri bowed slightly.

Talib rested on another bed nearby, his stick gun beside him.

Nouri sat down beside him, saying, "How are you?"

Talib shrugged. Like A'mma Fatima, he looked as white as a piece of *samoon* bread. His curly hair was stuck to his forehead and he didn't look Nouri in the eye.

Without thinking, Nouri pulled the Game Whiz from his pocket. The dark screen still lit up with flashing lights, pings, and tiny blasts. He thrust it at Talib, saying, "Here. It's yours now."

But Talib just stared.

Nouri sighed. Talib had been through a real bombing, and here he was handing him a miniature war. But he had nothing else to give. "Please take it," he urged.

When Talib continued to stare, Nouri set the Game Whiz down next to his feet, saying, "I'll come back soon. We'll play a game together."

CHARRED

When the muezzin called the next morning, Talib heard al-Shatri's radio playing, the announcers telling and retelling the awful news.

Baba beckoned to Talib. "My books," he said softly. "Go. Get them." And he closed his eyes.

Talib glanced toward the window. "Of course, Baba."

"I'll go with you, Talib," said Mama, reaching for her head scarf.

Talib thought of taking his stick gun, of holding it across his chest as a real soldier would. But he knew the gun was just a child's toy and today he had a man's work.

Warm, smoky air filled the stairway, and Mama pulled her scarf across her face.

At the bottom of the stairs, no one tended the tea maker's stall or the stand of silver bracelets. Fires still smoldered in boxes of books and in the innards of wrecked buildings. Talib covered his nose with a handkerchief against the dirty curtain of ash. Mutanabbi Street had become the Gray Zone.

Talib looked up at al-Shatri's building. Two of the columns supporting the upper story had been blown away. Much of the ornate facade lay in a heap.

A man passed, muttering, "Allah is great!"

But how could Allah have let such a thing happen?

Two men were unreeling a wheel of barbed wire. Two others stretched the wire across the front of a building that tilted precariously.

Talib and Mama stepped through the wreckage, some pieces taller than they were. An unwound black turban, now a long cotton ribbon, lay over a twisted metal book cart. There was a smashed violin, children's stickers, a pair of shoes, and honeyed baklava ground into the sidewalk. Here and there something dark stained the sidewalk.

A charred cell phone lay beside a bit of burned flesh. A note attached to the phone read: "This is the only remains from this person. Everyone is going back to Allah."

Mama let out a sob.

Scavengers with black garbage bags picked through the rubble.

At the corner, two Iraqi soldiers blocked the way.

"No sightseeing," one said roughly.

Talib stepped in front of Mama, shielding her. "We're not sightseers. We have a bookstall here. We need to get our books."

The soldiers glanced at each other, then stood aside.

"I wish we could go back home," Mama said, wiping at her cheek.

"We will, Mama," said Talib.

"I mean to Karada."

He took her hand, repeating, "We will."

Talib hardly recognized the spot where the bookstall had once been. He could barely make out Baba's red carpet, black now, littered with debris and with large holes burned in the wool.

Mama knelt down and began to cry, covering her face with both hands.

Talib offered her his handkerchief. "Don't, Mama. It will be all right."

The shelves of books, once protected behind the plywood, were now a heap of charcoal. Some of the books which had been displayed on the carpet still looked readable. Others still smoldered, plumes of smoke spiraling slowly upward.

"Let's put the ones that can be mended in one pile, like this." Talib set a book on the edge of the carpet. "And the ones that are too damaged in another. Over here."

In silence, Talib and Mama sorted, sometimes hesitating over which pile a book belonged in, sometimes quenching a pocket of burning embers. They coughed and their hands grew black. When Mama wiped her cheek, she left a black smudge.

Talib lifted a book and put it here. Lifted another and put it there. Each book seemed impossibly heavy. He wondered who had done this terrible thing to Mutanabbi Street? How could anyone, Shiite or Sunni, have done this?

At last the books were laid in two piles: those thoroughly charred and those less so. Talib looked up at the street, blanketed in smoke.

"Let me look around a little, Mama," he said. "Afterward, I'll carry the good books upstairs."

"Not today, Talib. Don't look around today."

"I need to see what's happened," Talib protested.

"Then be careful." Mama stood up, straightening her skirt, her head scarf. She touched his cheek with the back of her hand.

He watched as she walked down Mutanabbi Street, avoiding the rubble. He made sure the two soldiers let her pass.

When Mama had slipped out of sight, Talib began his old route. Everything was completely unfamiliar now. Many buildings had shattered glass and holes blown in the walls.

At the spot where the Shabandar Café had once risen against the blue sky, the blades of a ceiling fan poked through a pile of bricks. Talib thought he spotted a black-and-white photograph lying next to a broken teapot. He walked closer, peering into the wreckage.

An Iraqi policeman shouted: "Stay back!"

At al-Nakash's stall, Jabir paced the sidewalk, stepping over scraps of Martin Luther King, and bits of pretty Marilyn Monroe mixed with the torn-up face of Ali Bin Abi Talib, cousin of the prophet.

An ambulance sat parked on the street nearby, the lights flashing. Talib watched two men loading a stretcher. He looked closer. Was that *al-Nakash* on the stretcher? The man had al-Nakash's round face and pursed lips.

"Al-Nakash!" Talib cried.

"No use calling him," said Jabir.

"Is he . . . ?" A shudder ran through Talib. His hands froze around the edges of the canvas.

Jabir nodded.

Talib watched as al-Nakash disappeared inside the ambulance. The men slammed the doors shut. How could Allah . . . ? How?

Jabir, his jaw working, tears streaking his ash-covered face, said, "See! Something has to be done."

"But what?" Talib asked.

"We need to get back!"

"Get back at whom?" Talib asked.

"It doesn't matter. Get back at anyone."

As the ambulance pulled away, Jabir ran after it. He banged on the back door until the driver stopped and let him in.

Coughing with smoke, and half tripping, Talib fled in the other direction.

. . .

He brought armload after armload of Baba's books into their little room, his knees trembling with exhaustion, his mind trembling with Jabir's words.

"Thank you, my son," Baba said as each load arrived.

Talib brought with him the smell of burnt paper, the new smell of Mutanabbi Street.

BIG GUNS

Nouri woke to Baba's voice: "Nouri! Stay away from the windows!"

He sat up sleepily, but then his eyes opened wide at the sound of gunfire. He rushed into the front room to see Baba standing to one side of a window, pulling the curtain back, peering out. Mama had barricaded herself behind a table turned on its side. The tablecloth lay puddled on the floor. A vase had shattered. Mama clutched a wailing Shatha.

"Come here," Mama ordered, moving to make a spot.

"But—" Nouri gestured toward Baba.

"Come right here," she commanded, her silver bracelets clattering.

At a volley of gunfire, Shatha screamed and Nouri joined Mama behind the table. But he insisted on looking around the edge of the table toward Baba.

"There's men out there I've never seen before," Baba was saying. "They're shooting at each other, throwing rocks, bottles."

"I wish you'd get down here with us, Mohammed," pleaded Mama.

But Baba stayed by the window.

Baba wore his security guard gun in a holster at his waist. Every now and then he rested his hand on it. Baba said he'd never shot the gun. Not once.

Would Baba go out to join the fight?

Nouri wished Mama would let him stand with Baba, checking out the action.

"These men aren't anyone we know," said Baba. "They're making Karada a battlefield. All for their own purposes."

When gunfire hit the house, even Baba crouched. Nouri covered his ears. Would the bullets strike the windows and come right inside? This felt nothing like playing war with his cousins.

During lulls in the fighting, Shatha slept and even Nouri dozed, his head propped on the table leg. Over and over, he woke to renewed gunshots.

As the light reddened with dawn, there came a new sound, like the purr of a giant cat. The gunfire slowed. There were a few pops, then silence.

Baba took a longer look outside. "It's the Americans," he said. "They've brought their tanks."

Nouri rushed to the window before Mama could stop him. Outside the street was filled with green tanks, their big guns rotating this way and that. Helicopters beat the air.

Right by the window, there came the sound of many feet running.

When all was quiet except for the drone of the tanks, Baba opened the door.

Nouri stood behind him on tiptoe, looking out into the dusty air.

After a period of quiet, Baba led the way through the courtyard.

Nouri followed, leaving Mama and Shatha peering from the doorway. He ran a quick eye over A'mmo Hakim's car in the courtyard. To his relief, it stood undamaged, as if the night's events had never happened.

When Baba opened the gate, Nouri looked out. By the wall of the white bougainvillea, where he and his cousins had played war, two men lay sprawled.

"Dead," Baba whispered.

There was no way to tell if the men had been Sunni or Shiite.

At that moment Zaid al-Najeeb came out of his house. He lifted his arms to the sky, declaring, "They will have to kill me! I will never leave!"

Baba groaned.

...

Nouri didn't ask permission to go visit Talib on Mutanabbi Street. Surely, Mama would object. Instead he slipped out. As Nouri walked to the bus stop, past the tanks, he picked his way over shattered glass and splashed blood.

...

At al-Shatri's, Nouri burst in: "There was a gun battle right on our street. Two guys got killed. Right where we used to play."

Talib's eyes widened. "You're joking."

"It's not a joke." Nouri kept his hands behind his back, not wanting Talib to see the way they still shook.

On Talib's tiny balcony, the boys surveyed the scene below. Barricades kept out all vehicles except American tanks, police cars, and dump trucks. Dark banners floated overhead, mourning the dead. The scrape of shovels filled the air as men loaded rubble onto wheelbarrows and trucks.

"It isn't right for people who don't even live in Karada to come fight there," Nouri said.

"Are there any Sunnis left?"

"Only al-Najeeb. You remember him? The mechanic?"

"Of course."

"He's acting crazy. Someone's going to kill him."

"Mmm," mused Talib.

"We should do something." Nouri gestured toward the blackened, smoldering scene below.

"But what?"

Nouri noticed a small cut over Talib's eyebrow and suddenly couldn't bring himself to speak. Really, Talib had been through much more than he had. He picked up the Game Whiz from a nearby table, saying, "I'll hold it, but you can press the button on that side. I'll do this one."

It felt good to have his hand so near Talib's, and to do something together, working as a team.

A SUNNI

As Talib reached the broom high into the corner, searching out spider webs, the radio made an announcement. The man's voice clearly stated that the noontime attack on Mutanabbi Street had been carried out by an *irhabi* Sunni. The *irhabi* Sunni had driven the car with the bomb inside. Like little soldiers, his words marched into the air.

Talib beat at a mat of webs. So a Sunni had finally avenged those marauding Shiites. The ones who'd broken the neighbors' windows and stolen refrigerators. The ones who'd shunned him and Mama.

But then he set his broom against the wall and sat down on a stool. A Sunni like him had set off the car bomb. A Sunni had destroyed great beauty. A Sunni had injured and killed innocent people, including al-Nakash.

Without a word, al-Shatri brought Talib a cup of tea.

The radio announcer went on to talk about growing strife in the neighborhoods of Baladiyat, Saidiyah, Doura, Hurriyah, Ghazaliya. . . .

Now even Mutanabbi Street was no longer a haven. In all of Baghdad, no safety remained.

. . .

"They say Mutanabbi Street will be closed for months," said Baba that afternoon. "If I can't sell books, what are we going to do here?"

Talib looked up from his book. He was reading about the dancers, Nasirulla and Salma, who'd stolen their master's gold and escaped. He put a marker in the page. "Can't we just go home?"

Mama began to cry.

Baba laid his hand over Talib's, saying, "Yes, someday. But not yet."

They had no home. They had nothing but damaged books. Still, the books were everything. Talib gestured toward the boxes. "Should we try to fix those?"

Baba nodded. "Might as well." He stood and gathered a roll of tape, a bottle of glue, and a small soft brush. He pulled up a chair at the worktable, saying, "With the war, we have no cookies or baklava. Books have to be our sweets."

When Talib brought over the first book, and Baba flipped it open, a small cloud of dust fanned into the room.

Talib sneezed.

As the two of them made their way through a short stack, cleaning some, fixing others, their fingers grew black. The soot, Talib thought, was the sorrow of Mutanabbi Street. How could something so broken be fixed? Why had he suggested such a thing?

Al-Shatri came into the room, rubbing his hands together in their fingerless mittens. He took up a book and read: "When the Mongols sacked Baghdad in 1258, the Tigris ran red one day, black the next. The red was the blood of the victims. The black the ink of the books."

"See, Talib," said Baba, "it's worth our time to repair these. Iraq has a great tradition of literacy."

Talib smiled. Books were the bread of Baba's soul.

"Let me help," said al-Shatri, pulling up a stool.

The three of them worked in silence, handing the books back and forth. In the end, none was perfect, but all could be read.

When it came time to light the kerosene lamp, Mama set out their little blue bowls, and then brought out the lentil soup, steaming from the stove.

After they'd washed the soot from their hands and pulled the clattering stools to the table, Talib realized he'd worked for hours without thinking of anything but books. Mama's lentils tasted good and he ate up his bowlful quickly. The kerosene lamp threw a halo of light onto the small blue flowers of the tablecloth.

Just as they finished eating, the muezzin's evening call sounded—holy words floating into the sky. Mama went to the corner and unrolled her prayer mat.

But Talib stayed seated, tapping his fingertips on the edge of the table.

"You never pray anymore," commented Baba.

"I can't," Talib responded.

"Allah can be a refuge in hard times," said al-Shatri softly.

Talib nodded, noticing that al-Shatri wasn't praying either.

"This war is not Allah's fault," al-Shatri added.

Talib nodded again. But Allah was still supposed to be all-powerful.

"Pray with me, Talib," Mama urged, preparing for her ritual washing.

Talib shook his head. No.

CAR GREASE

In the morning, a crowd had gathered in front of Zaid al-Najecb's garage.

When Nouri went over, he saw al-Najeeb stretched out, blood flowing from a bullet hole in his head, his hands still black with car grease. Someone had stepped in the blood and tracked it up and down the sidewalk.

Nouri looked up at a row of pigeons balancing on the electric wire.

SUMMER

ME?

One scorching afternoon, Talib and Nouri lay side by side on the floor, the coolest place. They had positioned themselves in the line of the fan, so that it blew straight on them, stirring the hot air.

"There," Talib pointed to the ceiling. "I see marching camels. And a cave filled with treasure. Or there," he gestured toward the wall, "Arabs battling Persians."

"I don't see any of that."

"Nothing? Not even the camels?"

"Maybe a woman with long hair."

The fan rattled and Talib leaned up on one elbow to take a sip of water.

Pushing his hair off his damp forehead, Nouri said, "Shiites are moving into Karada. Into the abandoned Sunni homes."

Talib drained his glass. "The ones who came to fight?"

"Probably not. These don't look like fighters. Just ordinary people. Families. Maybe Shiites who got kicked out of their Sunni neighborhoods."

"What about *our* house?"

"Someone's in yours too."

Talib tried to imagine a Shiite mother in Mama's kitchen, a strange father wiping his shoes on the mat, a strange kid in his bed.

Someday Baba would reclaim the house and they'd move back in. In triumph, they'd kick out those Shiites.

With a slow clatter, the fan stopped turning.

"Darn," said Talib. "The electricity's gone off."

The air now pressed around them like warm bread dough. Talib considered getting up, soaking cloths to drape across their foreheads, but even that effort felt like too much.

Talib half imagined, half dreamed that one of the camels on the ceiling came to life. He was riding it across burning dunes. . . .

"You know I . . ." Nouri began. "I . . ."

"You what?" Talib prompted, his eyes wide, his body thrumming, wondering if, finally, his cousin would admit what he had done.

"Nothing."

Talib sat up. "Were *you* the one who threw the rock through my window?"

Still on his back, Nouri spread both hands, as if showing he held nothing. "Me? How could you think that? I was asleep at home that night. It wasn't me. I'd never do that to you."

"Liar," Talib muttered, lying back down.

ROOFTOP

In spite of the nightly bombings, Nouri helped Baba maneuver the cotton mattresses up the narrow stairway to the roof when it got too hot to sleep inside. "I'd rather die of a bomb than perish in this heat," Mama had said.

Baba swore mightily whenever the mattresses got stuck.

Lifting from the bottom, Nouri bore the weight, his fingers pinched.

When they emerged on the rooftop, the sun burned like a giant kerosene flame, searing the sky, turning it the palest of blues. Even the stiff fronds of the palm trees drooped, weighted down with heat and dust.

Nouri gazed down at the street below where Talib had stolen the soldier's helmet. Where Sunnis and Shiites had fought.

If there was another gun battle, they'd at least have a good view from the rooftop.

And there, looking like a toy, sat A'mmo's black car. One of the tires was flat now. Just that morning, in spite of the heat, Nouri had washed it using a small pail of water. No one ever drove the car anymore—gasoline was too expensive.

Baba stared down too. "Time to sell that car. I'll talk to that dealer over where the bus makes the turn toward Buratha."

Nouri turned away.

. . .

"This is like a party!" Shatha exclaimed.

It *was* like a party, Nouri had to admit as they gathered around bowls of dates and pitchers of yogurt. He could hear neighboring families laughing and talking on their rooftops. The sound of a reed flute wound its way through the pink air.

As the sky darkened, music floated from a distant cabaret. Mama sang along to the recording of the Egyptian singer, Umm Kalthoom, so famous she was called Star of the East.

When Shatha leapt up and pretended to sing into a microphone, Jalal and Anwar laughed.

"She's just showing off," muttered Nouri.

Baba stood up and turned his back on Shatha. "I wonder how my brother's family is doing," he said over the top of Shatha's singing. "I wonder if they're partying."

Shatha dropped the hand that held the imaginary microphone. Everyone stopped talking. No one looked at anyone else.

Nouri stared down at the red roof tiles.

Finally, everyone lay down and examined the night sky. There weren't as many stars as in the countryside, but a few glittered through the branches of the *nabog* tree. The night sky revealed omens: would the future be full of health and bounty or did danger lurk?

Talib had always been the best at the game of seeing things in the sky. Playing at being a fortune-teller, he'd predicted: *You will marry a woman with dark eyes. . . . Beware of an overly friendly man. . . . Large amounts of gold await you. . . .*

"I see a monster," said Jalal. "That star is the eye and the little group there makes the body. . . ."

"A shooting star!" shouted Anwar.

"That was tracer fire," corrected Nouri.

"Was not."

Nouri struggled to stay awake as long as possible. Whenever he closed his eyes, he thought of A'mmo Hakim.

One spring day, A'mmo had taken him to Mosul. Although the car had air-conditioning, they'd rolled down the windows. With the warm wind blowing through, A'mmo had driven fast, barely missing the donkey carts and the slow buses, while Nouri had laughed with nervous excitement.

But he mustn't think of such things anymore. A'mmo Hakim had been dead nearly a year now. Nouri forced his eyes wide open.

Suddenly he saw three stars lined up like a sword. He covered his heart with both hands. It was the sword of destiny. The stars were about to make him pay for what he'd done. The sword plunged straight downward, aimed at his very center.

AUTUMN

RAMADAN

During the holy month of Ramadan when the veils of illusion parted, it was said that a person could perceive Allah most clearly.

Talib fasted, not out of devotion, but because there was little to eat. He thought not of Allah, but of his empty stomach.

How could he think of *Allah*? Allah had betrayed him. Thoughts of all that had happened hurtled through his mind. How could Allah have permitted those things?

...

The ban on foot traffic on Mutanabbi Street had been lifted, though there were still barricades against vehicles.

"Why don't you open your bookstall again?" Talib asked Baba.

"No one will come," he replied. "They're still afraid."

"If there are books, people will come," said al-Shatri from across the room. "Someone has to make a move. Someone has to be brave."

Baba lifted his hands, but then just dropped them back onto his knees.

"Yes, Baba, why don't you?" said Talib. He gestured toward the books that he and Baba had repaired.

"Books are Iraq's only hope," pressed al-Shatri.

"That's true," Baba said, nodding. "I will go down tomorrow." He looked at Talib, his eyebrows raised in a question.

"I'll go too," Talib said quickly.

· · ·

The next morning, Baba and Talib rose early and carried books to the street.

"Take this too," Mama said, tucking a small broom under Talib's arm.

When they emerged from the stairwell, the tea maker was boiling water in spite of the heat. The silver bracelet seller nodded in greeting.

The men who'd once gathered in the Shabandar Café now sat at cafés on the sidewalk, dressed in white shirts, sheltered by striped awnings.

Baba's bookstall spot was littered with rubble, burned bits of books, and pigeon droppings.

"It needs a good cleaning," he commented.

"That's what the broom's for," said Talib. He chased the large pieces of debris into the gutter, and then the dust.

When the area was clear, Baba squatted down beside the books. He left them in the boxes, the spines facing outward so that the titles were clearly visible.

Meanwhile, Talib hunted for bits of abandoned wood to make a new storeroom, new bookshelves. He found some scraps behind a crumbled wall. He found a piece of tin for a new door.

As Talib explored an abandoned building, a nail poked through the sole of his shoe and a cloud of dirt fell on his head. He stood looking around, away from the noise of the street. Not long ago, this had been a bustling shop. Now the place reminded him of the cave where the legendary boy, Rejab, had lived.

He felt something soft underfoot and touched a carpet gingerly with his fingertips. Baba could use a new carpet, even if it did need a lot of cleaning. Talib paused a moment longer, imagining an escape from his own life, coming to live in a place like this, like a character in a book.

When voices from the street roused him, Talib pried up one edge of the carpet and yanked on it, dragging the load.

"Look what I found, Baba!"

Together he and Baba spread the carpet flat. As Talib swept it, triangular designs began to appear, woven with yarn that had once been white.

Talib moved the boxes of books onto the carpet. He brought over a wooden crate for Baba's seat, announcing, "Now we have a real bookstall."

Baba smiled. "You've done enough, Talib. Go on now."

"You'll be all right alone?"

"I can handle the crowd," joked Baba, gesturing toward the mostly empty sidewalk.

When Talib glanced back he saw a man in a red shirt leaning down to stare at Baba's books. With luck, perhaps he'd buy something.

He headed to where al-Nakash had once had his magazine stand. On getting closer, he shielded his eyes from the sun. The stand was there again—

with magazines piled high on the tables! Jabir stood nearby, his hands clasped behind his back.

Unlike his father, Jabir didn't bustle about, helping customers find a rare magazine. Instead he stood, his eyes slits, using his pocketknife to whittle a piece of wood.

He wasn't making anything, Talib decided. He was just using the knife.

. . .

Two weeks later, the crescent moon was sighted again, bringing an end to the month of Ramadan.

In the days before the war, Mama would have put away the cloth with the blue flowers and brought out the special one—pomegranate-red embroidered with gold. The long fast over, the table would once have been laid for the feast of *Eid al-Fitr*: lamb skewered with green peppers and onions; fava beans and eggs cooked in oil; grilled chicken, stuffed tomatoes, rice pudding, sesame cookies, candied citrus peels. . . .

Now Mama served lentil soup and hot cardamom tea.

But most importantly, every year when Ramadan ended, Talib had felt his connection to Allah renewed. He'd experienced a sweet confusion, a hazy melting into Allah's holy presence.

Now his relationship to Allah felt as stale as a piece of day-old *samoon*.

Talib was happy only that al-Shatri, while cleaning, had come upon a bag of sweet dried figs.

"IT WAS I."

Nouri and Talib squatted, taking turns at shooting marbles into a circle, competing to get closest to the bull's-eye center.

Nouri flicked a red *daa'bul* with his thumb, knocking Talib's green one.

"No!" Talib laughed, rocking back on his heels.

In his palm, Nouri clicked together three glass balls. Just then a breeze whirled the dust into a cone. The cone spun across the dirt lot, picking up bits of trash before crossing the *daa'bul* circle.

Without meaning to, without planning it—the words rushed out of his mouth on their own. "I did it.

It was I," he said to his cousin. He stared at the cone of dirt moving toward Mutanabbi Street.

"I know," said Talib. "I saw you shoot."

"Not this. I mean I threw the rock. Through your window."

Talib shaded his eyes, stared.

Nouri bit his lip and nodded. His lip tasted dusty. It was as if he'd shot a gigantic *daa'bul* and was waiting to see what it would hit.

Drawing back his arm, Talib raised his hand. The glass ball had struck home.

Nouri covered his face, preparing his body for the blow. He deserved whatever came. He waited. But there was nothing. He heard Talib stand up.

Peeking between his fingers, Nouri watched Talib kick all the *daa'bul*, one by one, across the dirt, still standing right next to him.

Then Talib lifted his foot and kicked him.

The blow landed in Nouri's ribs, and he couldn't help but scream out.

Talib shouted: "I knew it was you! I hate you! I don't ever want to see you again! Never! Never!"

Nouri scrambled up, holding his side. He backed away, his feet slipping over the scattered *daa'bul*. He held up his hands, protecting his face from Talib's blows.

Finally, Talib pushed him backward into the rubble. He fell hard onto something sharp, then lay still, listening to Talib's footsteps thudding away.

MEET ME AT DAWN

Breathing like a demon, Talib pounded his way through the bookstalls, by the *chai khana* and the bangle sellers and stacks of Winnie the Pooh cards. He ran through Friday shoppers, and around a corner displaying lumpy, tattered furniture. He almost tripped on a plastic flower. There was nothing to do but keep running.

At last, he slumped down against a ruined building. His body was exhausted, but his mind still burned. Nouri deserved more than a mere kick in the ribs, more than a few punches.

He had to be properly punished.

As his heartbeat slowed, Talib's thoughts turned to Jabir with his slitted eyes and rough face. Jabir had kept saying that he, Talib Jassim, should *do* something. As if he had something in mind.

Talib picked a hole in the knee of his pants. Should he approach Jabir? Jabir was so much older. Jabir might laugh at him, still just a child.

But it was worth a try. What a fool he'd been to play *daa'bul* with Nouri, to tell stories with him, to welcome him into his home. . . .

Talib made his way past the plastic flowers, around the old furniture, and through the Friday shoppers. He went by the *chai khana* and the bangle sellers and stacks of trading cards. He wove through the bookstalls, all without bumping into the Friday shoppers.

Finally, he arrived at the magazine stand where Jabir stood with a baseball cap pulled low, wearing sneakers with green laces.

Talib took up a magazine and pretended to study the black-and-white photographs of a group of rock 'n' rollers called The Rolling Stones.

Engrossed in a picture of a Rolling Stone slapping a whip onto the stage, Talib started when a shadow fell over the page. Not daring to look up, he let his gaze fall to Jabir's sneakers.

Jabir took a step away, the green laces undone, trailing in the dirt.

Gripping the magazine, Talib said quickly, "You say I should do something." His voice sounded tinny, like the voice of a little kid.

Jabir's exhale of breath was smoky. "Don't tear my magazine."

Talib set the magazine back on the stack. "I'm ready," he stated.

"Ready?" Jabir's tone was mocking.

"Yes."

Jabir scratched at his dark chin hairs. His words were like the flutter of the awning. "Meet me at dawn. Over there."

Talib looked up to see Jabir looking toward a building with dirty white columns.

"Now, go on," Jabir ordered. "Get out."

Walking back along the street, Talib thought of how Jabir had taken him seriously. A person like Jabir understood when a kick and a few punches weren't enough.

At al-Shatri's, he took the stairs two at a time, bursting through the blue door at the top.

"What is it, Talib?" asked al-Shatri. "What's happened?"

Talib's voice filled the room: "Nouri was the one. He betrayed me! Because of him, I live *here*!" Talib kicked a box of paper. "He was the one who threw the rock."

"*Nouri?*" Mama asked.

"Yes, Nouri. That *Shiite* Nouri."

"Talib," Baba said sternly. "Calm down."

But he couldn't. He didn't want to. His hands itched with the desire to hit Nouri again and again.

...

That night, Talib lay with his heart in a knot. He had an appointment with Jabir at dawn. In the daylight all had seemed simple. But in the dark, he sensed the rustling of danger.

Should he go?

What would Allah think?

Talib buried his face deep in his pillow.

...

Before the muezzin's call, before the sky turned rosy, Talib snuck out. He tiptoed through the room where the printer snored loudly.

He plunged down the stairs, marched into the street.

Someone grabbed his collar. "What are you up to?"

"I live here." Talib pointed in the direction of al-Shatri's apartment. He peeked behind him to see an Iraqi soldier.

The soldier released him, saying, "You shouldn't be out this early."

"My mother needs some tea from Rashid Street."

"At this hour?"

"She's sick."

"Go on, then." The soldier gestured with his rifle.

Talib ran toward Rashid, finding a crumbled wall to hide behind. He crouched until the air pinkened and the soldier had disappeared. Then he doubled back.

He spotted Jabir leaning against the column, wearing plaid pants and a white T-shirt.

Jabir lifted his hand briefly, then pushed aside a broken metal gate. He gestured toward the inside.

Gradually, Talib's eyes grew used to the darkness. He made out great blackened rolls and the darting of rats. Rusted mesh and chunks of concrete poked through the thin soles of his shoes.

When they reached a stone slab, Jabir sat down and reached into his pocket for a pack of cigarettes.

Talib took his place on the stone, keeping his distance.

Jabir tapped one end of the cigarette against his thumbnail, then lit it. "So what is it you want?"

"My cousin Nouri . . ."

Jabir held up a hand, exhaling smoke through both nostrils. "I don't care about details. What do you want to *do?*"

Talib took a big breath. "I want to get back at my cousin."

"Really?"

In the gloom, Talib sensed Jabir examining him. He swallowed hard. "Really."

A truck passed by, and the building shook. Talib glanced up at the trembling ceiling.

Jabir rapped the stone slab with his knuckles. "Then it's simple. I can teach you. Throw it and *whamo!*"

"But that might *kill* someone," Talib protested. He glanced at the light coming from the front of the building. How long would it take to get away?

"But I thought you wanted to get back at him."

Talib shook his head. He imagined hurling a gasoline bomb at Nouri's house. It might go through a window as the rock had. Or it might sail over the wall to land in the courtyard with the dry fountain. Into A'mma Maysoon's house of Friday feasts. Blasting her glass room of orange trees and pigeons. "I'm not sure . . ."

"Hey! Who's in here?" called a rough voice.

The silhouettes of two Iraqi soldiers appeared, their rifles aimed into the darkness.

For once, Talib was glad to see soldiers.

"We're just talking," Jabir replied.

"This place is off-limits."

"Get out!" said the other soldier, gesturing with his rifle.

Talib stood first, followed by Jabir, who lazily stretched as he stood up. They retraced their steps through the building, the soldiers following.

Outside, Talib blinked in the sunlight.

"Same time tomorrow," Jabir said so quietly that Talib wasn't sure he'd heard. "Over there," he flicked his index finger toward what had once been a spice shop.

Talib gave a tiny nod.

Yet hurrying back to al-Shatri's, he vowed never to meet Jabir again. He could never create a bomb, much less throw it at his family. What had he been thinking?

Upon entering the apartment, Talib couldn't help but notice the way al-Shatri saved bottles. A line of dusty empties was lined up along the wall beside the bags of round white onions.

HEAVIER

There was no way that Nouri could walk normally with the large bruise on his side. Talib's kick had been bad enough. But then he'd fallen down hard on the spout of a metal teapot when Talib had pushed him.

"Why are you walking like that, Nouri?" Mama asked.

"I fell off a wall. Jalal and I were playing war."

Mama rolled her eyes. "I don't know what kind of fun that is with real war all around us."

Nouri shrugged.

"Let me take a look. Maybe I can put something on the wound."

But with both hands Nouri pulled his shirt down tight. He didn't want Mama to see. Besides, he felt like he deserved the pain of the bruise.

But his confession hadn't released the weight of his burden. The heaviness of what he'd done had only grown worse.

SPICES

The next morning, Talib went to the abandoned spice shop after all. He reasoned that if he didn't go, he wouldn't be able to face Jabir. And here on Mutanabbi Street, he couldn't avoid him.

He didn't go on time, however. He arrived after the muezzin had called twice.

Stepping into the murky darkness where sacks of cardamom and black pepper lay broken open, he sneezed.

"Jabir?" he called in a whisper, and then louder: "Jabir!"

No one answered. A rain of dust fell from the ceiling.

Finding the shop empty, Talib let out his breath. To make up for being late, he decided to wait.

The sacks lay like sleeping animals, and Talib paced among them, trying not to breathe the spices. He knew he shouldn't get mixed up with Jabir. His ideas were insane. In his wildest fantasies, Talib had never considered becoming a *bomber*. He didn't hate Nouri *that* much.

Looking out the small window at the back of the shop—the glass broken—Talib recalled a time when he and Nouri had been about six years old. Nouri had traded his reed flute for a chance to ride an older boy's bicycle. When the teenager had immediately ridden off, laughing, the flute tucked under his arm, Nouri had cried.

Talib had offered a pack of gum from his pocket. Together they'd chewed it, peppermint filling their mouths, devising a plan to get Nouri's flute back.

This dirt lot outside the window was where he and Nouri had played with the *daa'bul* not long ago. He leaned out, cutting his finger on an edge of broken glass.

To forgive Nouri wouldn't mean he had to go see him. It didn't even have to mean being friendly. But for now he wouldn't do anything crazy. He'd wait until he moved back to Karada, and see how he felt then.

...

Talib strolled over to the magazine stand. He'd say his father had kept him on business. If Jabir pressed him to meet at another time, he'd look him straight in the eyes and say he'd changed his mind.

At least he'd *try* to say that.

As Talib approached the stand, his pace quickened.

But only a bald, paunchy man stood behind the magazines, under the striped awning.

"*Marhaba*, A'mmo," Talib said. "I'm looking for Jabir."

The man shrugged. "He left last night. Didn't say where to."

"He's gone then?" Talib smiled. What good luck! Jabir had missed their meeting too.

The vendor shrugged again. "With that boy you never know."

WINTER

ORANGES AND BOMBS

The winter oranges ripened in Mama's glass room, glowing like small suns. Each morning, Nouri pulled one off a branch and tore into it. As he bit into the sweet flesh, the juice squirted into his face.

Nightfall brought the usual battles between Sunnis and Shiites. While the gunfire ricocheted off nearby buildings, Nouri arranged and rearranged his collection of Japanese trading cards. No longer did Baba watch curiously from the window, nor did Mama cower with Shatha behind the table. All four slept in the bedroom at the back of the house, far from the street, used to the sounds of war in the night.

One morning Nouri went into the courtyard to find a large bullet hole in the windshield of A'mmo's car. The impact had caused the glass to spider web.

Nouri bit his lip and looked away.

Although Baba had talked to friends about buying A'mmo's car, no one had enough money.

Nouri should have felt glad that the car was still theirs. Yet it had been a long time since he'd polished it or sat behind the wheel. The car, which had once reminded him so sharply of A'mmo Hakim, now sat with all four tires flat, the once-glossy finish splattered with pigeon droppings.

A BLUE TAXI

Slowly, many of the booksellers returned to Mutanabbi Street. Every day, two or three more set up
shop. Baba chatted with his old friends, comparing
stories of hardship.

Every day more galleries and cafés opened. Banners
flew again. Rock music pounded the air. Men hauled
books from one stall to another, their carts clicking.

More and more shoppers ventured onto Mutanabbi Street, clutching the collars of their winter
coats. Whenever anyone stepped onto the carpet of
white triangles, Baba smiled and spread his hands,
saying, "Look. Please look." Still, later he'd complain,
"Their wallets are so empty."

Warplanes crisscrossed the sky and Mutanabbi Street trembled with distant explosions.

Whenever Talib ventured to the magazine stall, he saw only the older man whom he now guessed to be al-Nakash's brother. Talib hoped that if and when Jabir returned, he'd have forgotten they ever talked.

Talib noticed that every day a blue taxi parked in a small side alley. The driver spent his time drinking tea in the *chai khana*, and the door to the gas cap was missing.

He noted this out of mere curiosity, he told himself. He didn't really care that the taxi driver was practically *offering* him free gasoline. He was just observing.

Yet when he came upon a short length of rubber hose, he picked it up and tucked it carefully under his coat.

FIERCER

That night's battle was fiercer than usual, with no relief in gunfire. Even sheltered in the back bedroom,
Nouri heard bullets pinging against the front of the
house.

Shatha climbed from her spot on the floor into
Mama and Baba's big bed. Nouri wished he could
climb in too. But he didn't feel like sleeping so near
Baba.

Whenever the bombs burst, Nouri sensed the
three in the bed above flinch. Even Baba flinched.

Sometime after midnight, a plane zoomed overhead, droning like a gigantic insect. Then came a
huge blast.

Nouri froze, waiting, his fingernails plunged into his palms.

After a few minutes of silence, he whispered, "We're still here."

"Praise be to Allah," Mama whispered back.

"Praise be," echoed Shatha in her small voice.

Only Baba remained silent.

NEVER

Talib had settled himself on the wooden box, ready for a day of bookselling, when Baba said, "You'll need to work alone this morning."

"Why, Baba?" Perhaps Baba was off for a long chat with one of his old friends.

"I've heard news about Karada. I'm going back there."

"What news?" Talib sheltered his eyes from the cold sunshine, looking up into Baba's face. Was the news good? Was it now safe to go home?

Baba's gaze drifted to a spot somewhere beyond the ruins of the Shabandar Café. He drew his eyebrows together. "A bombing."

As the words exploded in the cold air, Talib jumped to his feet. "I have to go with you."

Baba shook his head. "Another time."

"No, now!"

Baba rearranged his red scarf. "There's been heavy fighting in Karada. Last night the battle got so out of control that the Americans brought in a plane and bombed."

"A bombing could end all that fighting."

Baba grunted, looking down at Talib. Then he bent down and placed a stack of books in a box. "If you're coming, we'll have to pack up."

. . .

The bus driver was still suspicious; the red vinyl seats were still dusty. The Tigris River looked drier than ever.

Talib leaned his forehead against the cold window glass. What would he and Baba find in Karada?

At last, Baba signaled the driver to let them out and they descended the steps. Once the two halves of the door had closed behind them, Talib looked around. Debris littered the streets. Red and black graffiti, pocked with bullet holes, screamed from the walls of buildings and homes.

Three American tanks rolled slowly down the street, rubble popping under the great treaded tires. An ambulance roared past, driving halfway up on the sidewalk.

As they walked, Baba kept looking over his shoulder. There were a few others out, but Talib recognized no one.

Instead of going straight, Baba turned right, as if to avoid Nouri's house.

Two more turns and they'd come to the two-story tan building with the blue trim and the narrow gate. How would he feel to see other people's laundry on their line? To maybe get a glimpse of a stranger through their windows?

Suddenly Baba stopped.

"What . . . ?" Talib started to say. Then he choked his words back.

This was his street. But there was nothing. Nothing.

The whole block had been knocked down. Burned. Even his two-story tan building with the blue trim and narrow gate. Even the persimmon tree outside the kitchen window. And Mama's jasmine bush. Masses of wilted bougainvillea lay over the fallen walls. The row of palm trees stood, but with blackened fronds.

A group of American soldiers tramped through the rubble, talking quietly among themselves, their guns at their sides.

Talib looked behind him. This couldn't be his street! Baba must have taken a wrong turn.

But Baba was crying out. He held both hands to his head and cried out.

A cold hand gripped Talib's heart. This *was* the right place. This *had* been his home.

He would never live here again.

"I'm going to find Nouri!" Talib shouted, turning away.

"Talib! Stop!" Baba gripped his arm. "Nouri is in school."

"I'll find him there!"

"Talib! *Nouri* didn't do this. . . . This wasn't his fault."

"But . . . but he . . ." Talib's mind filled with a red fog.

Baba held Talib tight until his hot sobs died away.

Walking back to the bus, they came across a lump of burned cloth. Poking at it with his foot, Talib discovered the stars and stripes of an American flag.

. . .

Back on Mutanabbi Street, Talib—hands clenched—went again in search of Jabir. Jabir's idea was wild. But it was the only idea left.

At the sight of Talib, the older man shook his head at him. "He's still not back."

"Thank you, A'mmo," Talib said, then turned away. Really, he didn't need Jabir, after all. He already knew what to do.

. . .

When al-Shatri wasn't looking, Talib grabbed one of the empty bottles from the collection. He smudged out the clean circle it left on the dusty floor and moved a bag of onions to cover the empty spot.

He tucked the bottle into a spot between his mattress and the wall.

. . .

And yet, Talib still waited for Jabir. He didn't want to get this wrong.

He visualized making the bus ride all by himself. But he wondered if his arm was strong enough to throw the bottle far enough. And he worried that he might be seen.

When he really thought about it, Talib was horrified by the idea of hurting or killing anyone. But sometimes he didn't think about what would happen when the flaming bomb hit its target. He thought only of his joy in finally doing something, of the moment he would let the bomb fly.

At last, on a day of cold wind and a bitingly blue sky, he caught sight of Jabir standing guard under the awning of the magazine stall. He wore a scarf wound up around his ears and he hunched against the chill. As Talib drew close, Jabir busied himself with rearranging the magazines.

Talib flexed his fingers in his mittens. "I need help," he said.

"You haven't *done* anything yet?" Jabir asked, straightening a stack. "What are you, a little coward?"

With the toe of his shoe, Talib shoved a pebble back and forth. "I just wanted to be sure of exactly what the . . . what it . . . you know, looks like."

Opening a magazine, Jabir took out a pen. He looked around. Then, over an advertisement for a sleek car with fins on the back, he sketched a bottle, drew wavy lines inside it, and then added the rag stopper. Finally, laughing, he drew a picture of a lighted match. Moving the magazine close to Talib, he said, "Throw it quickly so you don't become a martyr."

"Some people choose to become martyrs," said Talib.

Jabir stared at him. "Are you ready for that?"

"Not . . . no . . ." But Talib thought of how the martyr at Buratha had been a young boy like himself. Was he prepared for such a fate?

"I have no money for the bus."

Jabir sighed, searched his pocket, and finally handed over some coins. Then he ripped out the magazine ad, crumpled the page, and tossed it away into the cold wind.

. . .

At dusk, the blue taxi was parked in its usual spot, the driver nowhere to be seen. For a few moments, Talib stood looking up and down the alley: no one. Quickly, he knelt. At last, the hose swished against something.

Talib sucked and got a mouthful of burning gasoline. As he spit it out, the pale pink liquid flowed through the hose and into his bottle.

As he waited—the hose was quite narrow— memories of Nouri flickered through his mind. Once he'd gone with him to A'mma Maysoon's family farm in Mosul. That warm morning it had been their job to kneel in the soft soil, pinching three leaves off each watermelon plant, leaving the fourth to grow fruit. He and Nouri had worked elbow to elbow.

Toward noon they'd scared off a small brown snake.

At the end of the day they lay together in the field as dusk gathered, pink at the edges of the sky.

Maybe he wasn't so angry with Nouri after all.

But then Talib thought of the wreckage that had once been his home.

At last the bottle was full and Talib took a rag from his pocket. He was stuffing it into the neck of the bottle when someone called out, "Hey, boy, what are you doing?"

Talib looked up to see the taxi driver, waving his cap, dashing toward him.

He hid the bottle under his coat and ran down the alley, passing a group of older boys playing soccer.

When he looked back, the driver was nowhere in sight.

Working his way along the side streets, he arrived back at Mutanabbi. It was too late to go to Karada today. He'd get on the bus late afternoon tomorrow. Once in the neighborhood, he'd hide out until nightfall.

Meanwhile, where should he store the bomb? He couldn't take it home—not with the strong smell. He thought of the spice shop, which had its own pungent odor.

He located the shop, looked both ways and entered the gloom. Once inside he felt the sacks with one hand, clutched his deadly burden with the other. Finally, he plunged the bottle deep into a bag of cinnamon sticks.

THE LIGHT OF ALLAH

The winter days had grown colder and more bitter than anyone could remember. Mama stuffed towels around the window, but the icy wind still found its way in.

The sky hung low, the clouds like wet cement.

Because of the war, there was no electricity. There was no kerosene for cooking, to heat water for tea or to fuel the lamps. While Mama and Shatha huddled in blankets, Nouri collected a pile of rocks in the corner of the courtyard. If the gun battles got close, he wanted to be ready.

Sometimes Nouri peeked down Talib's street. Bright laundry hung from the lines that squatters had strung in the ruins. Once he heard flute music. It sounded like a trickle of cold water.

…

That January night there was no battle. Nouri lay awake, listening to the quiet. The wind, normally sharp, blew like a caress against the windows.

He relaxed into that soft wind, as if into a pleasant dream. Was this A'mmo Hakim coming back to him? Was this Allah's grace?

An idea drifted in, as if carried by the breath of the wind: he could make up for the harm he'd caused. He could give the black car to Talib's family. On Mutanabbi Street, A'mmo Nazar could probably sell it.

The next day Nouri would propose the idea to Baba. He'd polish the car until it shone with the light of Allah himself.

THE WHITE ZONE

Allah is great! The recorded voice of the muezzin called at sunrise. *Allah is great! There is no God but Allah!*

Talib rubbed his eyes.

Instead of getting up, Talib burrowed deeper into the blanket, his breath fogging the cold air. Today was the day he'd sever his connection with Allah forever.

He'd hidden the bus money in the pocket of his coat, along with three wooden matches. That afternoon he'd retrieve the bottle from the bag of cinnamon.

Talib pressed his face into the pillow. He had only enough for a one-way bus fare. How would he get back to Mutanabbi Street? *Would* he get back? And what if someone had found the bottle of gasoline? What if the bus driver smelled the gasoline on his coat? Picturing the explosion, he squeezed his eyes tight.

Because his coat reeked of gasoline, he'd left it on the stairs. What if someone took it, along with the money?

Talib threw back the blanket to find the room unusually chilled and damp. The light had dawned pale, as though rain was falling. If it was raining, surely he couldn't go to Karada.

At the window, he wiped the condensation from the glass, then blinked in surprise.

This wasn't rain, but something else. Something like white cotton. It drifted onto the roofs of the buildings opposite, onto the palm trees. It floated all the way to the ground.

Below, on Mutanabbi Street, people stood gazing into the sky. They raised their arms, as though to embrace the whiteness.

Talib snatched up his wool cap, calling, "Mama! Baba! Look outside!" He ran to the room where the printer slept. "Al-Shatri! Look outside!"

On the stairwell, he grabbed his coat and ran down the stairs. He burst into the street to stand with the others, lifting his face, his hands. This white rain fell so lightly, so slowly. He had no word for it.

"Mama! Baba! Al-Shatri!" he called up to the windows.

Soon Mama and Baba emerged from the stairwell, supporting each side of al-Shatri.

"Look!" cried Talib.

Al-Shatri took off his fingerless mittens. He let the flakes fall onto his open palms, exclaiming, "In my eighty years, I have never seen such weather!"

"It's so quiet," said Mama, glancing around. "It's never so quiet."

It was true. Today there was no rat-a-tat-tat sound of gunfire. No explosions of mortar shells. The city was holding its breath.

The white kept falling, sticking to the ground like a lacy veil. It covered the chaos left behind by the bombing. Talib wondered if it was covering his blackened home in Karada.

When he reached down and pinched up the fluffy whiteness, the cold stung his fingertips.

The world was moving in slow motion. More people came onto the street and smiled upward. More silent flakes fell.

. . .

"Jabir!" Talib called.

Jabir had emerged from an empty building, blinking. He waved at Talib, then took off his baseball cap, catching the flakes.

Talib imagined people all over Baghdad venturing outside, gazing into the falling white. Talib imagined Nouri standing in his courtyard beside his uncle's black car, the white flakes settling on the glossy surface.

He thought of the bottle of gasoline, that deadly concoction, stored in the bag of cinnamon. How could he have ever thought to throw such a thing?

The new world was like the white page of a book. The world was like a page with no words, a page ready to be written upon.

A new page in which the war had stopped. In which no bombs fell. In which no guns were shot.

There wasn't a Green Zone. Or a Red Zone. There was only a White Zone.

"This is a message from Allah," declared al-Shatri. "We must end this war."

Talib nodded. Al-Shatri was right.

"Allah has sent a white miracle," whispered Mama.

"He's quenching the fires of war," Baba said.

The delicate white flakes settled on their wool caps, on Mama's head scarf. They caught in Talib's eyelashes.

Yet the miracle wouldn't last forever. As soon as the day warmed a bit, all this beautiful white would be gone. The miracle was only a message.

Looking up at the sky, which was dropping not bombs, but white flakes, Talib understood that he had to end his own war. Somehow he had to let go of his bitterness toward Nouri.

Allah was covering everything in the same white blanket, showing mercy for all. He wasn't on the side of the Sunnis. Nor of the Shiites. Allah was on all sides.

Allah was reaching out for him, and Talib had to reach back.

He took up a long stick. Balancing it carefully, he wrote in the delicate white layer that had fallen:

الله اكبر

[Allah is great!].

It wasn't the appointed time for prayer. No muezzin called from the minaret. But suddenly, Talib knelt and bowed down. He bowed down to Allah, the one as close as his own breath, the light of the heavens and earth. He pressed his forehead to Allah's white miracle.

AUTHOR'S NOTE

From 1979 to 2003, Iraq was ruled by Saddam Hussein. Hussein relied upon tactics such as torture, murder, and imprisonment to maintain his hold on power.

In 1991, the United States fought the first Gulf War against Hussein after he invaded the small nearby country of Kuwait. Though he lost the war, Hussein remained in power.

In 2003, the United States again went to war against Iraq. This time Hussein lost control of the country. The dictator went into hiding, was captured, and finally executed by Iraqis.

Hussein's fall from power was not the end of the conflicts. As a Sunni Muslim, Saddam Hussein had oppressed the rival Shiite Muslims during his brutal reign. After his fall, the balance of power changed and violence flared between the two sects.

Without an effective police force or an army to control the old hatreds, fighting became rampant. Lawlessness spread.

Unfortunately, the war was not only between armies. Iraqi civilians also took an active role. People who had once been friendly neighbors ostracized each other. In an atmosphere of terror, neighbors bombed and shot members of the opposing sect.

One place, however, seemed a refuge from the ravages of war: Mutanabbi Street. This street was the intellectual and artistic heart of Baghdad, flourishing with cafés, galleries, and booksellers. People drank tea, smoked water pipes, and talked politics. On Mutanabbi Street, no one cared who was Sunni and who was Shiite.

Tragically, in March 2007, this peace came under attack. A car bomb exploded in the heart of Mutanabbi Street. The explosion killed thirty-eight people, smearing the pavement with blood. Smoke rose from the burning books. The famous Shabandar Café and other historical buildings were destroyed.

Those who had loved Mutanabbi Street were devastated.

Then in January 2008, a miracle took place. Snow fell in Baghdad for the first time in anyone's memory. This wondrous act of nature achieved what the warring factions could not. During the hours of snowfall, a small truce came about. Weapons were silenced and no blood was shed. In the midst of a long conflict—one that is still ongoing in 2012—this snowfall provided a small measure of healing.

GLOSSARY

A'mma—aunt, term of respect for older females

A'mmo—uncle, term of respect for older males

A'nba—pickled mango syrup

Baba—father

Chai khana—tea shop

Daa'bul—a marble

Dolma—grape leaves, tomatoes, eggplants, or zucchini stuffed with rice

Eid al-Fitr—feast which ends Ramadan

The Green Zone—the center of Baghdad where the U.S. occupation forces live and work.

Hafiz—a Persian poet and mystic who lived in the fourteenth century

Infidel—a non-Muslim

Irhabi—suicide bomber or terrorist

Marhaba—hello

Mihrab—an archway in a mosque which faces Mecca

Minaret—tower on a mosque from which the muezzin calls

Muezzin—man who calls Muslims to prayer five times a day

Nabog—a tree with edible white or purple berries

Ottoman Empire—this empire lasted from 1299–1923. At its height it spanned three continents, controlling much of southeastern Europe, the Middle East, and North Africa.

Pacha—soup made of lamb's head

Quzi—roasted and stuffed lamb

The Red Zone—the area immediately outside the Green Zone.

Samoon—an Iraqi form of pocket bread

Sana Helwa Ya Jameal—Happy Birthday, Handsome

Shiites—a branch of Islam that believes the Muslim saints, godly men who commit good deeds rule the community, should be the blood descendants of Muhammad. Shiites will pray only on the earth, which is made by Allah.

Sunnis—a branch of Islam that believes living Muslims should be able to select the Muslim saints themselves. Sunnis will pray on man-made surfaces.

Yabsa—white beans cooked with tomatoes

ACKNOWLEDGMENTS

I would like to thank Professor Shak Hanish for his anecdotes, for his tidbits of Iraqi culture, and for his careful vetting of the manuscript. I am also grateful to my agent, Kelly Sonnack, and to my editor, Andrew Karre, for their faith and guidance.

ABOUT THE AUTHOR

Known as an "ambassador to children around the world," Carolyn Marsden voices the stories that most need to be shared with young readers. Carolyn Marsden's debut novel for young readers, *The Gold-Threaded Dress*, was named a Booklist Top 10 Youth First Novel and a Booklist Editors' Choice. Since then, she has earned starred reviews and other accolades for her novels set around the globe. Carolyn has an MFA in Writing for Children from Vermont College. Visit her online at www.carolynmarsden.com.